# The Magical Tea Shop

# The Magical Tea Shop

*Charmed Love Romance*

Aimee O'Brian

The Magical Tea Shop

Copyright© 2025 Aimee O'Brian
Tule Publishing First Printing January 2025

The Tule Publishing, Inc.

ALL RIGHTS RESERVED

First Publication by Tule Publishing 2025

Cover design by Erin Dameron-Hill

No part of this book may be used or reproduced in any manner whatsoever without written permission except in the case of brief quotations embodied in critical articles and reviews.

This is a work of fiction. Names, characters, places, and incidents are products of the author's imagination or are used fictitiously. Any resemblance to actual events, locales, organizations, or persons, living or dead, is entirely coincidental.

ISBN: 978-1-965640-66-1

*Dedication*

For Brian, life with you is magical!

Thou who loveth,
Be blessed amongst us.
With breath bestoweth
Thy heart.

The Hazard Blessing 1776

# Chapter One
*Not everything starts out magical...*

IVETTE WAYLAND CAUGHT her breath. With the sun shining down on him, Jaxon Langford always caught her just a little unawares. He only lived upstairs, but every morning she found herself anticipating his first appearance of the day. She gazed through the plate glass window of her cozy tea shop as his little black Scottie dog scampered to keep up with his long strides. Jaxon halted just outside her door.

*Would he enter?*

She ached to run her fingers through that molasses-brown hair, still damp from the shower and sparkling like sugared ginger crinkles. It was ridiculous how much she yearned to touch him. He was her landlord, for goodness' sake. Ivy reined in her longing. Jaxon paused on the sidewalk and quickly stepped over to hold open the door for the tiny, elderly Hazel Bestwick, president of the Hazard Historical Society.

*Please come inside, Jaxon.*

A couple of young boys on their way to school, backpacks swinging, asked him a question. Jaxon leaned down to answer. He fist-bumped the taller of the two boys and grinned. Jaxon's smile shot straight to her core. As if sensing her watching, he glanced at the window, trying to see through sunlight bouncing off glass, his eyes the color of a well-steeped Irish breakfast tea.

She let out a little sigh. What she wouldn't give to have him for…

"Focus," said a voice behind her.

Ivy jumped and blinked twice to bring herself back to reality. "You have customers. Remember your goals."

Her older sister's constant criticism put her on the defensive. Ivy swung abruptly to face her, causing her high blonde ponytail to smack her own cheek. She shoved it back. "Business is steady."

"*My* business is steady." Holly drew herself up straighter in her pink bakery smock smoothing a hand over her flawless updo before sweeping an arm out to draw Ivy's attention to the nearly empty tearoom. "*Your* business is slow. And he…" She flapped her hand toward the window "…is a distraction to success. You can't have it all. I keep telling you."

Ivy sucked in a breath and bit her tongue. She gazed out over her cute little tea shop with its small round tables covered in emerald-green tablecloths and ivory lace, topped with glass to protect the fabric from spills. Chairs with curved metal backs and comfy vinyl seats, reminiscent of a 1950s ice cream parlor, were mixed in with dark, bentwood chairs that might grace any Irish pub. Ruffled lace curtains framed her large window with its stunning view of the town square. Honestly, she couldn't hope for a better location. Her little Welcome/Shut sign in Old English script added that homey, yet elegant, note.

Of course, Hollister's Bakery, her sister's business adjacent to hers with its sleek modern design, had a steady stream of customers, while the Ivy Way Tea Shop did not. She could swear Holly popped over several times a day through their shared kitchen just to gloat. Holly's success versus her own less-than-success resulted in their ongoing argument.

*Was it possible to have a love life while building a successful business?*

Even though Ivy currently had neither, she believed that yes, it was possible to have it all. Holly maintained that it was not. Choices must be made. Priorities must be set.

Ivy turned toward her sister, losing sight of her delectable landlord as he strode down the street toward his own corner office. "*All* being a successful businessperson in a long-term relationship..." Ivy trailed off. She couldn't share her complete thought, *leading to my own personal happily ever after*. Holly would scoff. "Yes, of course it's possible, lots of people do it."

Holly rolled her eyes, and in one quick motion raised a hand to smooth her tightly coiled bun again. "Pu-lease. In this town? Who?"

Ivy opened her mouth to shoot back an answer, and faltered. Hazard did rather live up to its name in the romance department. Still. "Our parents."

"Who no longer live here."

"Well, what about Garrett and Priscilla?" It irked Ivy to name her high school nemesis, but Priscilla did seem to have had success in the romance department.

"Committed? They should both be committed the way they bicker. I would hardly call them happy, what with all her scheming."

"Okay." There must be happy, successful couples, but Ivy's mind was coming up blank. All she could think of were local relationships that had ended in divorce or tragedy. "Well, if it's what I want."

Holly pursed her lips, tilted her head, and shrugged. "Sure. Okay."

Ivy narrowed her eyes. Her sister never just agreed with her.

Holly continued, "You just can't have it *all* at the *same* time. Once you've achieved a suitable level of success, *then* pursue a relationship. If you want to build your business, little sis, put more effort into marketing instead of mooning over Jaxon Langford every time he walks by."

It was true that he did walk by a lot, since Langford Architectural Enterprise was just three doors down. She often saw him passing her shop window when he was going to meet clients. Plus, he walked that jaunty little dog twice a day.

"It's not like he's over his wife." Holly's words were like a drenching dash of icy, cold water.

"She's been gone three years," Ivy muttered. *Three years I've been waiting for him to see me as more than a tenant. Three freaking...*

"Success takes work."

Ivy let out a huff. Like she didn't know that. Still, Hollister's Bakery was busier than the Ivy Way Tea Shop by far, and Holly worked constantly. Her sister actually adhered to a ten-year plan. Amazing, really. Ivy preferred living in the moment, making the most out of each and every day. "Let's make a bet." The words fell from Ivy's mouth before she could reconsider.

"You'll lose."

"Not this time."

Holly smirked. "You always lose."

"So what are you worried about?"

"Hmm, I'll bite." Holly took a bite of a scone sample from the glass counter. "What do I win when you lose? And how do we know when you've lost?" She waved the remaining bit of scone in the air.

Ivy pursed her lips. "By the end of the month, I'll increase my business 30% *and* be in a committed relationship."

"And this is why you lose." Holly laughed and popped the last bit of scone in her mouth.

"It could happen."

Holly rolled her eyes. "In twenty-eight days? Your timeline's too short, with too many indeterminate variables that'll burn you."

Ivy resisted the urge to stomp her foot, or better yet, stomp on Holly's foot like Holly stomped on all her dreams. "Tell you what, if you win, I'll clean and close up your shop for a month and if I win, you'll clean and close up mine."

It wasn't fair, of course. Holly's bakery mess was much worse than Ivy's tea shop mess, but it didn't matter because this time Ivy would win. She glanced at the heirloom cookie press hanging from its emerald-green ribbon in a place of honor on her wall.

What if it wasn't just a myth?

What if the stories were true?

What if fate was just waiting on her to take the chance?

It might even be fun. Ivy loved fun.

With a nod, Ivy breezed past her sister to where Hazel Bestwick was seated with the other three members of the Hazard Historical Society, Ivy's favorite customers. If anyone would choose to be in her corner, it would be that crew, four pillars of the community who believed all things possible, and one of whom was her great-aunt Lydia. Like Ivy, the outwardly austere Lydia loved fun.

Ivy arrived at the table in time to hear Hazel's snarky view on their latest hire. "She's the unfortunate embodiment of her name. Would lightning strike her if she smiled? Who wants a tour with a downer docent?" Hazel's eyes glinted, daring her cronies to contradict.

"Lots of people," said Marjorie Hopewell, whose positive outlook and bright copper curls, courtesy of Cece's Salon for the last twenty years, kept the historical society on track. "Malory Stone's tours are informative, her delivery concise, and they are exactly one-hour long. I joined a tour of Oleander House just last week, and she did a marvelous job. Honestly, she could do a marvelous job for you, too, Hazel, if you'd just write down your script. Then you wouldn't have to give all those tours of your Gilded Age Mansion all by yourself."

Hazel harrumphed and fluffed her white, lavender-tinted hair. "I like giving tours of Sundial Sands. I'm not ready to retire." She peered through her spectacles at Ivy, her expression begging for a change of topic.

Ivy graciously handed out her list of specials. "We have fresh-baked chocolate chip scones today"—she smiled at Seymour Throckmorton who gave a nod, causing his shock of white hair to rise and fall with the motion—"along with cinnamon rolls from next door and my very own ginger molasses crinkles." Ivy closed her eyes for a moment as an image of Jaxon flashed through her mind.

"Ooh, I love those," said Hazel. "Do you have a new tea blend for us to try? The last one, well." They all exchanged a pained glance.

Ivy winced. Tea blends were an art she had yet to master. "I do. This one is a mint Darjeeling blend with a touch of rooibos. My Darling Mint To Be."

They exchanged another glance. Marjorie's bright smile faltered a bit. "You might want to work on the name."

"Just bring some of everything," said Hazel, eyes bright in anticipation at an imminent selection of treats. "And I'm certain you'll create the perfect tea blend yet."

Ivy nodded and hesitated, not sure how much to share of her conversation with Holly and the daring idea she'd just had.

"What is it, dear?" asked her aunt, her back ramrod straight. Her short, pixie-cut hair was colored the same walnut brown it had been her whole life.

Ivy opened her mouth, then lost her nerve. "I'll be right back." She scuttled away, doubting the wisdom of bringing them in on her plan. What if they weren't discreet? The entire town could be laughing at her by sunset, and then there would be Holly's inevitable scorn. She chewed her lip as she assembled their order. She needed another opinion, or several.

Should she confide in them? Would they think her absurd? Did it matter?

Holly retreated back into her side of the storefront to assist her employees with filling orders. The bell on Holly's shop door chimed and chimed again, with a constant influx of customers coming in to buy doughnuts and bear claws and loaves of sourdough. If Ivy didn't sell Holly's apple tarts and cupcakes in her tea shop, would she have any customers? Really, who couldn't make their own pot of tea? Still, the scones and cookies were her own unique recipes which she didn't share with Holly. The scones especially, served with clotted cream, were a local favorite and made the tea party experience special.

Ivy chose a pink-flowered teapot in a sage-green cozy. She organized it all on a gleaming silver tea tray with a matching sugar and creamer, and arranged the cookies, cupcakes, tarts, cinnamon rolls, and scones on white paper doilies. She gave a nod of approval at the presentation, quickly gathered up the tray, and carried it out to the corner.

"You always arrange everything so prettily," said Marjorie. She gave Ivy a sweet smile. "What's on your mind?"

Ivy blinked. Was Marjorie a mind reader?

"Yes, share with us." Hazel's eyes followed Jaxon Langford through the plate glass window as he made a second lap, walking his dog round the town green. She tapped her lips with a forefinger, as they curved up in a little smile.

Were they all mind readers? Or was she just that obvious? Might as well spill it.

"I made another bet with Holly."

Lydia scowled. "Ivette darling, I hate that you always lose those bets." She gave an exasperated sigh. "What is it this time?"

Ivy took a big breath, "That I'll improve my business by 30% *and* be in a committed relationship."

"That doesn't sound so hard," said Seymour. "I could fix you up with my grandson, Rory."

Ivy barely refrained from rolling her eyes at the thought of trying to schedule a date with a rock-band keyboardist, let alone one who was forever on tour.

"It's not Rory she wants," hissed Hazel. "He's never here." She turned her attention to Ivy and said cannily, "That handsome landlord of yours should be renewing your lease soon."

"Yes," said Ivy. This group was way too intuitive. "I plan to keep the tea shop going."

"What's the timeline on your bet?"

"End of the month."

"Definitely doable," said Marjorie.

Ivy loved Marjorie Hopewell. She was the embodiment of her surname.

"What's your plan?" asked Aunt Lydia, ever practical.

Ivy's eyes wandered over to the cookie press on the wall.

"Oh," they said in unison, followed by a reverent moment of silence.

"Is it true what they say about Hazard? Is our town really magic?" asked Ivy.

"Well, I don't know about magic. It's the blessing that makes Hazard special," said Hazel.

"Speaking the blessing over an object imbues it with power," added Marjorie, as she stirred a third spoonful of sugar into her tea.

"That cookie press brought love to your parents and has kept them happily together for decades. They share a batch of those cookies each year on their anniversary. They're still like honeymooners while they cruise round the world performing their little magic shows." Lydia smiled at the memory.

"Tell me the promise," Ivy said to her aunt.

"You must know it by heart."

"Please."

Lydia's eyes took on a faraway cast. "The antique cookie press, handed down through generations of our family, when combined with the proper recipe, infuses so much love into the cookies, you'll win the devotion of the recipient."

"Who's the recipient? Your customers? Is that how you plan to improve your business? Good idea," Seymour nodded in approval. "I'll keep coming back." He took a big bite of his scone.

Marjorie's eyes sparkled. "Yes, that must be it." She took a delicate sip of her over-sweetened tea before adding another generous dollop from the shiny sugar bowl Ivy moved closer to her. "It couldn't have anything to do with…"

Ivy cut her off. "What do you think? Would it be fun?"

"Oh, it would definitely be fun." Lydia clapped her hands.

The four pillars nodded in solidarity at Ivy's plan.

"You should do it," they said in unison.

# Chapter Two

IVY WAS LOCKING up her shop at the end of the day when Holly popped her head in.

"You want to just start now, cleaning up for me? It would save time." Holly grinned.

"Shoo," said Ivy. "Your place is all cleaned already. I know it is. You closed up an hour ago, and you're an organizational neat freak."

Holly laughed. "Let's just say I look forward to winning." With a wave, she headed out. Ivy could hear her cheery little bell jingle jangle as she locked her front door. She watched as Holly walked across the street to her white bakery van with its jolly, bubble-gum-pink writing on the side, advertising Hollister's Bakery everywhere she went.

Holly knew how to market her business. Ivy could probably learn a thing or two from her sister, but she liked doing things her way, growing her business organically. Maybe her business didn't expand as quickly, but it was manageable and met a need in the community. The perfect place for shoppers to stop in and take a break, it fit right in with the Hazard Historical Society's plan to draw tourists from nearby

Newport, Rhode Island's many mansions and experience Hazard's own four unique mansion tours.

Ivy made sure her sister got in and drove off before she reached up and removed the antique cookie press from the metal hook on her wall. She stroked the bright green, velvet ribbon and held the cookie press reverently in her hands. She murmured the blessing, her fingers tracing the edges of the swirling floral design. The press did make the loveliest cookies. She remembered her parents sharing them and laughing. Every year on their anniversary, they would bake them together and go on a picnic at Cliffside Park. They always ate all the cookies themselves, never sharing a crumb. It was why Holly started baking at twelve, making red velvet cupcakes for her and Ivy to share.

Ivy sighed. They both missed their parents, who were happily sailing the Mediterranean.

With a deep breath, Ivy moved to the special drawer in her antique hutch where she preserved her secret recipes. They were family heirlooms, really, handed down through the generations. And they had been gifted to her, not Holly. She found this remarkable because Holly was the baker and the eldest.

"You'll not be burdened by limitations," her mother had said as she placed three weathered, hand-written journals in her youngest child's hands. "So, these are for you, because you are a believer in all things winsome and wild."

She'd just turned eighteen. She hadn't realized the importance of the legacy her mother was bequeathing her, not then. But she'd been pleased and honored to be singled out, to be chosen over her sister for once. Her parents hadn't meant to favor their oldest child over their youngest, of course, but Holly demanded attention in the way of overachievers, while Ivy watched from the sidelines.

But her mother knew Ivy loved their family history. How her maternal ancestors had traveled to Hazard, Rhode Island, from Normandy, France, in the mid-1700s and settled here, while her father's ancestors had come from Ireland to America a century later to escape the potato famine. She adored knowing that her parents had met at a charity fundraiser on the same town green that sat right outside her shop window.

Hazard was home. Ivy gazed out at a pink-tinged sky, dimming into dusk over the little town square. She loved the placement of her own little business, snugly between Hollister's Bakery and LaFleur, her aunt's crowded and sweet-scented flower shop. Her gaze wandered approvingly over the other local businesses: Leo's diner, now managed by his stepson Pedro, which served everything from hearty breakfast specials to lobster rolls; Throckmorton Grocery, still managed by Seymour himself, the first in a chain of corner marts that now graced a dozen little towns in the Northeast, each store run by a family member; Community Projects, a thrift shop that supported local charities because this was a town where the residents looked out for each other; The Hazard

Inn, with its For Sale sign, ready for a new owner to come and remodel it back to its former glory—no small task, that. And on the far end of Main Street sat Langford Architectural Enterprise, next to Cece's Salon. Ivy couldn't see those from her window, but she knew Jaxon would be seated at his desk, doing whatever it was architects do.

Her eyes settled on the imposing granite statue of Captain Hazard in the middle of the town square. Ever solid and reliable, the captain was surrounded by elaborate white benches in the center of a lush green lawn.

Giving a decisive nod, Ivy picked up the darkly burnished skeleton key for the one special drawer she kept locked in her country French hutch. She held the key, coolly resting in the palm of her hand, savoring this moment before she slid it into the lock. She turned it until she heard the tiny click. With a rush of breath, she slid her very special drawer open and stared at the jumble within.

Unlike her sister, she was not an organizational neat freak.

She knew the recipe she needed was in the oldest journal, the one at the very bottom of the drawer. And while the drawer might appear disorganized, she remembered the order of the contents, as she had arranged them herself with the oldest journals tucked into the bottom and the newest ones on top.

The recipe for today, the Very Special Recipe as per the legend, was only to be used in dire circumstances. At least that was how she interpreted it. Desperate times called for quantifiable measures, and she would accept that challenge. Ivy needed Jaxon Langford to see her, really see her.

Was he still mourning his wife? Ivy shook her head. He didn't act like a grieving husband. Jaxon took on work projects, played community baseball, and coached Little League. Surely, he had moved on with living his life. And, perhaps, he didn't always want to be alone.

Ivy was ready to live *her* life to the fullest. What was she waiting for? She couldn't be governed by her sister's negativity. She would do this.

She eased out the oldest journal. With care, she turned the brittle pages. She ran her finger over the curling script. She *should* type up these old recipes and store them on her laptop, but she loved the spidery writing from some early ancestor, copied over and over through the decades, the original pages no doubt long since turned to dust. The recipes were kept legible. The careful preservation of the smallest details made what she was about to do all that more profound.

Ivy smiled, confident now. She was most at home when she was baking. She spread the recipe flat and ran her index finger down the list of ingredients. Next, she gathered the items to arrange in a loose semicircle on the counter. Flour, baking soda, salt. Measuring carefully, she stirred them together in her favorite mixing bowl before setting them aside.

The wind picked up. Ivy glanced up, surprised to see the red maples in the square start to move with a breeze that had come out of nowhere. Next came the sugar, ginger, and cinnamon. She softened butter, holding it over a stove burner, before working it in with a wooden spoon. She didn't want to use her mixer tonight. She wanted to prepare the recipe as closely as possible to the original.

Wind gusted, rattling her door like an insistent visitor. Ivy frowned. Odd that, the weather report had been mild, she was certain.

After combining the soft ingredients, she carefully cracked three eggs, breaking the yolks and folding them into the sugar mixture. While her door rattled itself into a frenzy, she hand-whipped the batter smooth.

Ivy bit her lip. She was so, so tempted to add in nutmeg. Nutmeg made everything better. You couldn't go wrong adding nutmeg, not to cookies, but it wasn't listed in the recipe. She reached for it and hesitated. Her hand trembled. "Must resist," she murmured. "Must follow recipe exactly." Besides, if she was going to add it, it should have been added with the other spices. If she added it now, it was out of order. She worried her lower lip with her teeth.

She rather liked out of order.

Holly hated out of order. If Holly had these recipes, she would follow everything flawlessly.

Ivy wasn't flawless. Not ever. But tonight was different, right? Tonight was about desperation and longing for Jaxon to see her for who she was, so she needed to follow the rules. Maybe following the rules would tip the odds in her favor. Her thoughts churned along with the gales outside.

Scalded scones! She really wanted to add the nutmeg.

Her hand shook, reaching out of its own volition. Sighing, she pulled it back. This project would only work if she made the recipe exactly as it was. Those were the rules. Still, having to follow a recipe precisely was bothersome. Improvisation in life was essential.

She pressed her hands on the countertop. She could hear her sister's voice in her head, giving her instructions just as she had through their childhood while her parents were practicing their pretend magic. Holly saw improvisation as a flaw. Holly proclaimed improvisation in baking reprehensible. Holly was successful.

Fine, she would follow the rules. Success, too, would be hers.

A strong blast hit the building, rattling the windows and door sharply, repeatedly, like it was desperate to enter. The overhead lights dimmed once. Ivy held her breath and let it out when they stayed on. The branches of the maple trees on the green waved wildly, leaves breaking free, swirling loose in uncharacteristic gusts.

Ivy stopped, fairly vibrating with how much she wanted to add the nutmeg. She blew out a breath. She couldn't do it. She just couldn't.

She could not… "Okay, admit it," she said. "Following a

recipe exactly is impossible. I can't do it. I can't."

Rule following to that degree simply wasn't in her.

She huffed out a breath, one sole tendril of hair around her face, fluttering.

"Oh, bother." She grabbed for the nutmeg, unscrewed the lid, and before she could stop herself, shook a generous smattering into the cookies.

This whole project was just for fun anyway, right? The blessing of Hazard was a myth. All magic was artifice. She'd learned this by watching her parents, professional illusionists, practice magic tricks at home.

Besides, nutmeg *would* make the cookies taste better.

She just hoped the power would remain on—she needed it to bake these cookies. Ruined cookies, possibly, as far as magic went, but they'd still be delicious.

*Was this all a waste of time?*

She mentally kicked herself. No, this is *for fun.*

She tilted her chin up. "I'm having fun. I'm in charge here." Baking cookies to win the devotion of the man she loved was almost cheating. She mentally slapped her forehead. Magic was not real. Fun was.

She mixed all the ingredients and set the batter in the walk-in freezer to chill. It needed to chill for two hours before she could roll it out. While she waited, she began to transcribe some of the old fragile recipes onto her laptop. She loved the one for stone-ground cornmeal biscuits. That sounded unique and was something she could use in her shop. Likewise, the one for beef barley soup with root vegetables sounded equally yummy.

Ooh, adding a soup of the day. That would be great fun, especially on blustery days that came out of nowhere. She rolled her eyes. Fortunately, the flurries died down and quit rattling the door. Time to stop fretting about the power going out.

Ivy typed up a dozen recipes, everything from roasted new potatoes with fresh dill to peanut soup, and checked on her dough. Time to roll it out.

She preheated the oven, washed her hands, and collected the dough from the walk-in. Carefully, she laid out parchment paper, then rolled and cut perfect circles of dough. The breeze picked up again, buffeting the building in gusts. It revved her up.

She developed a rhythm as she worked, timing her motions with each puff of wind as if working in tandem with some unseen force. Once the cookies were cut and set out on the baking sheets, she paused. With reverence, she washed and dried the cookie press. She held it in her hand.

This was the moment.

Ivy pressed each cookie with the intricate imprint and, following the recipe again, gave each one a fine dusting of cardamom.

Beautiful.

Her lights dimmed once, twice. Ivy held her breath. Would they stay on? If they went out now, this might all be for nothing. She crossed her fingers and counted to sixty. When the lights stayed steady for a full minute, she let out a sigh of relief. Okay, she could keep going. She murmured the blessing as she worked, figuring it couldn't hurt.

*Thou who loveth.* She thought about Jaxon and all his wonderful qualities. Really, they were wasted if he never set out to live a full life again. That was what she wanted for him. Yes, she was making these cookies, and winning the bet with Holly would be fun, but what she truly wanted was Jaxon's happiness.

*Be blessed amongst us.* She thought of all his contributions to the community from coaching Little League to community fundraisers. He'd even helped to design a gazebo pro bono for Cliffside Park.

*With breath bestoweth.* A sense of peace settled over her as she slid the first batch of cookies into the large oven. She used an hourglass with lines measuring each ten minutes. It, too, was an antique from her family. She kept careful watch on it as she worked.

*My heart.* This time she thought about how important it was to make her customers feel welcome by serving them comfort food and drink, the wind once again blasting the town outside. At the ten-minute mark, she pulled out the first batch. Perfection. She had a rhythm going now, and the weather served as an accompaniment. A peace settled over her once again as she worked.

*Thou who loveth,*
*Be blessed amongst us.*
*With breath bestoweth*
*Thy heart.*

Humming and making up a little song for the blessing, she smiled. Had it ever been set to music? She grinned. That was something she could share with the Hazard Historical Society. If anyone knew it would be them, and if it hadn't been done before, well, they would get a kick out of it. By the time she pulled the very last batch from the oven, the lights flickered once, twice, and out.

Ivy blew out a breath. She'd done it; she'd finished before the power gave out. She left her cookies to cool while she set out tea lights on little china saucers all around the kitchen, and cleaned up with only candlelight to see by. Once the kitchen was spotless even by Holly's exacting standards, she reached for an antique tin that her aunt had given her for her last birthday. It was black, with a gold fleur-de-lis on the lid. Ivy packed up the now sufficiently cooled cookies and neatly arranged them. They fit perfectly in the large tin. She worked the lid closed and just like that, the power blinked back on.

"Well then." Ivy gave a nod. She set the tin on a shelf, blew out her tea lights and put all the saucers away, carefully removing any of the evidence of her night of baking. She really didn't relish the idea of explaining to her sister what she'd been doing after hours.

Ivy locked up her little shop, ready for the new day. Which, oh dear, had already started. A glance at the sky confirmed its arrival, with bands of gold and orange heralding the new morn. Her sister's crew would be clocking in any moment to start their baking. Disinclined to provide an explanation as to why she was still in the shop, Ivy hurried to her car to drive home and catch a couple hours sleep.

# Chapter Three

"DID YOU DO it?" Seymour asked as soon as Ivy swung by his table and set down a frosted cinnamon roll on a little china plate for him. He always arrived promptly at eight, the others more inclined to straggle in over the next half hour.

Marjorie, her bright red hair newly styled in a chignon, popped in next and sat by Seymour. "Yes, did it work?"

Hazel came in chatting with Ivy's aunt Lydia. They settled themselves at the table, hands folded before them. It was 8:05. All four pillars turned their expectant faces up at her.

Were they holding their breath? "I only just baked the cookies last night. So, we'll see." Ivy gave a little shrug, even as her eyes drifted to the tin. Their gazes followed hers. "I haven't gifted them yet."

"Ah," they murmured in unison, veneration clear in the single drawn-out syllable.

"I made up a little song," she added.

The four looked at her blankly. Hazel blinked several times. "A song, dear?"

Ivy nodded. "You know, to speak the blessing while I

baked the cookies."

Seymour glowered, his bushy, white eyebrows pinching down and together. He leaned toward Lydia. "Is that allowed?"

Lydia shook her head. "I don't think so."

Ivy bit her lip. "Come on, hasn't the blessing ever been set to music?"

Hazel frowned. "You should be careful. Deviation could have unexpected consequences."

"Unexpected good? Or unexpected bad?" asked Ivy.

"Unexpected," said Lydia with a solemn nod, "is unexpected."

Seymour nodded sagely in clear agreement.

"Don't look so upset. Expected doesn't necessarily mean calamitous. It—could go either way," said Marjorie, with an over-bright smile.

Ivy widened her eyes. Tepid tea! Her rule-breaking propensities would be her undoing, but—*fun*, she reminded herself. None of this was really *real*, right? Fun was the important bit.

"Was it fun?" asked Lydia.

Ivy nodded and relaxed. "So. Much. Fun."

"Then it's good," said Lydia.

They all beamed.

"I'm sure it'll be fine, dear." Marjorie recentered the day's jaunty orange daisy in the center of the table.

"I'll just get your tea. Today's blend is black Irish tea

with blackberry leaves and pineapple skin. I'm calling it I Pine For You." Ivy scurried away as Holly said at her ear, "Question for you."

Ivy jerked. "Why do you do that?"

Holly gave her a blank look.

"Just pop in and scare me. You have your own business to run."

Holly's lips quirked in a sideways smile. "I like to check on yours. Your tea shop adjoins my bakery. We *share* a kitchen. What you do in your *little business*," she said in her lofty, patronizing tone, "reflects on my *very* successful business, which runs like clockwork. Everything in its place, all my employees working diligently."

"In fear of you cracking your whip."

"They're *employees*. I pay them to work hard and make it look easy. They like it. They take pride in a job well done."

"I do, too." Her eyes wandered to her tin.

Holly frowned. "So, what exactly *were* you doing here at four thirty a.m.?"

"Wait, why do you care? Were you spying on me?"

"My early crew of bakers saw you in your car."

It shouldn't matter what she was doing, but Holly was waiting, foot tapping just the tiniest bit to highlight her impatience. Aware of her sister's scrutinizing gaze but reluctant to share the truth, Ivy hedged. "I couldn't sleep, what with that crazy windstorm. I wanted to check on the shop."

"What windstorm?"

Ivy blinked. "That wild cyclone last night. It rattled the whole building and knocked little branches off the trees in the square. You can't have slept through that."

"There was no wind last night. I'm sure of it. The weather report was clear."

"Well, a storm gusted here at the shops."

"But not across town where we live. So, the question remains, how could you have even known?" Holly narrowed her eyes.

Ivy hopped into motion. "Sorry, I need to get this out to my customers. She hefted the tea tray for the historical society, overloaded with pastries of all kinds, along with a lilac-flowered teapot with a hand-crocheted tea cozy in deep violet. The cups rattled with purpose as she carried them out. She struggled a little, afraid she might drop the tray. But she didn't dare goof up with Holly's critical eyes on her. She'd never hear the end of it.

She plunked the tray down on their table, and Hazel twitched at the noise.

"Sorry, it's a little bit heavy." Serious understatement, that. "But I wanted you to be able to sample everything. We have several special offerings today." Seymour's eyes lit up. His weren't the only ones. Even Marjorie's eyes brightened at the selection of raspberry scones, glazed cinnamon rolls, and molasses crinkles. The four dived into the offerings with gusto.

"Love these."

"Oh, these are the best."

"Hum," said Hazel, with a mouthful of raspberry scone.

Ivy blinked. Had she said Yum, or Hum? "I'm sorry?"

Hazel swallowed and waved her arthritic hand. "Your tune, for the blessing, hum it."

"Oh, okay." Ivy started, made it through about three notes and stopped, trying to remember how it went. She started again and gave a nod as she hummed. Yes, she had it this time. Then, the tune vanished from her mind. "That's odd. I hummed it all last night. Now, I can't remember how it goes." She gave a pouty frown. "I guess I'm tired."

Seymour glowered in disappointment.

Ivy shrugged. "I'm sure I'll remember. I promise I'll share it when I do."

Lydia raised her eyebrows. "Could be a blessing thing."

"What do you mean?"

"Part of the mystique," said Hazel in a loud whisper.

"Inspired," said Marjorie. "I like that. I'll check the historical writings and see what I can find about singing the blessing."

"Quite curious," said Lydia, "My niece is special. She might be the very first to ever put the blessing to music. How delightful. Try to remember it, and we can make a recording of it for posterity."

"I don't think it's *that* significant."

But the pillars were nodding, beginning to argue as to

the best way to record the song she'd made up and whether to write it down as a score or record her singing it. Ivy left them to discuss the history of the blessing and argue about how exactly to set it to music.

She stumbled through her day, bit by bit, the tune floating in and out of her mind, but never enough to be able to share with anyone. By noon she had her second wind, and she'd given up on remembering the song, instead humming favorite show tunes about dreams coming true. Plans to expand her offerings at the tea shop filled her head. She loved the new recipes she'd typed up the night before. By late afternoon she'd prepped for the next day and planned to come in early. As she set up her menu board for Friday, she fretted about how concerned the pillars were with the blessing being sung. She was especially glad she'd said nothing about adding the nutmeg.

# Chapter Four

JAXON PACKED UP his work. After a full day of perfecting plans for a kitchen remodel, a site visit, explaining to a stubborn client why he couldn't demolish a weight-bearing wall, and several hours of invoicing, he looked forward to taking a job with an established firm where he'd get to design single-family homes.

Finally, he could leave Hazard in his rearview mirror. What a name for a town! He was beyond ready to relocate to Boston. Serving as Hazard's tragic figure was demoralizing. All those pitying glances at Leo's diner, Throckmorton Grocery, Hopewell Nursery. Why did no one expect him to move on with his life?

He'd caught the ill-concealed whispers. "Poor Jaxon, whose wife fell to her death." Oh sure, the outpouring of sympathy had helped him right after Candace died, but now? It stung. The community viewed him as broken.

He didn't want to be broken.

The one place he never sensed any pity was the Ivy Way Tea Shop. The lovely owner of the cozy shop made him feel welcome. He'd even started drinking tea just to have an excuse to go in. The scones didn't hurt a bit either, especially the blueberry ones. Those were the bomb. But the cheerful demeanor of the curvaceous owner was the real draw. He could spend hours basking in her sunny little shop, the focus of her green-eyed gaze.

The only hitch was that Ivette Wayland was a tenant. He needed to stick to business, and he needed to tell her he was selling the property. He'd had a generous offer from Derrick Cross, the managing director of the H.A.S. Homes, a man motivated to buy up property in Hazard, a Boston developer with plans. Money from the sale would fund Jaxon's move to city life because, let's face it, Boston would be a great deal more expensive than Hazard. Plus, his new salary would allow him to save enough to build his dream home. He'd improved his designs over the last three years. One day, he'd be able to afford the land where he could build.

For now, he needed to let his tenants know that they would soon have a new landlord. He especially needed to forewarn Ivy, because he knew she struggled to keep her business up and running. New landlords invariably raised the rent.

He'd put together a binder with all the pertinent information for his tenants. His commercial building had just gone into escrow. A few details remained, but he would likely be signing the final paperwork by the end of the month.

Jaxon glanced at the clock. He needed to get to his

community baseball game, but he had just enough time to pop into the shop downstairs. Ivy would still be there, tidying up. He was sure of it. He'd often watched her go through the motions of closing while he walked Montgomery around the square. It took a long time for Montgomery to walk all the way around on those short little legs, stopping to sniff and nibble up every dropped crumb from the diner or the bakery.

For now, the pup was settled in his little bed in the corner with his favorite chew toy, a plastic, purple kitten that squeaked every time he bit down. Jaxon had stopped taking him to ballgames. The little troublemaker always managed to wriggle out of his collar and chase the balls, one time tripping a teammate rounding the bases. Roman had sprained his ankle, they'd lost that game, and everyone had blamed Jaxon.

Jaxon headed down the stairs. The afternoon light was just right to allow him to see through the tea shop's plate glass window. He paused at the sight of Ivette Wayland.

The woman was perfection. Her honey-blonde hair was pulled into a high ponytail that bounced with her when she walked. She stepped lightly, almost like she was waltzing while she swept the floor. He bet that she'd be humming a cheerful melody as she worked.

He opened the door she'd not yet locked, in time to catch the last refrain from "Some Day My Prince Will Come," before she spotted him. She choked, a blush creeping up her face.

"Sorry, I thought you'd hear the chime on your door."

"Oh, no, that's Holly's door. I don't have a chime." She tilted her head. "Guess I should get one. Hope I didn't burst your eardrums with my warbling."

"Not at all. Listen, do you have a minute? I need to speak to you about some changes."

Ivy nodded. With a smile, she produced a pot of tea and a large metal tin that she carried out on a pretty tray to the center table, set with two high-back chairs. All the other chairs had been flipped up on the tables. It was almost as if she'd been expecting him.

She sat and began pouring into teacups, so he followed her lead. "Earl Grey, hot?"

"Your favorite." She gave him a soft smile, and he relaxed. She had that effect, like there wasn't anywhere he'd rather be. He pulled himself back to what she was saying. "So, I know we need to negotiate a new lease. Business is picking up for me. I expect it'll improve significantly by the end of the month."

Her hands moved swiftly and dropped below the table edge. Jaxon blinked. Had she just crossed her fingers? But when he looked again, she was sweetening his tea with two sugars just how he liked it and setting a white-on-white Lenox teacup in front of him. "I know you'll need to raise the rent, the way everything else is going up these days, and I don't mind." She grimaced a little before her expression smoothed.

Clearly she did mind, but this conversation needed to go in another direction. It was only right. "About that." Jaxon drew in a breath. Ivy smiled, and Jaxon forgot what he meant to say. Ivy took a delicate sip from her own cup. Jaxon's eyes landed on her delicate hands, her fingernails painted the palest shade of pink.

He cleared his throat. "So, the rent increase. Five percent," he blurted. It was what he expected her new landlord would do. Although they hadn't had that discussion, it's what his research indicated. Surely Derrick Cross wouldn't raise it more than that. He might go as high as ten percent, but it was a small community. All the businesses in the complex were small, local enterprises.

Ivy gave a little frown.

Jaxon blinked and shifted at the slight downturn of her lips. "Too high?"

"Hmm," her lips leveled out and tilted up on the side. "I was thinking more in line with half that."

"Oh." Half that might be an issue. She leaned forward. He got a nice eyeful of cleavage before he noticed that her smooth hands, adjusting the teapot, trembled a little. "Well, so, okay," he told her.

"Thank you," she graced him with that sweet smile. "We have a verbal agreement." She spoke decisively.

Jaxon nodded and drank his Earl Grey. Ah, well, it would be Derrick's problem, he supposed. He *should* speak up. He knew it, but couldn't bring himself to contradict her. That tremble in her hands had cinched the deal. Selling should not put his tenants out of business. He just wanted out of Hazard. Jaxon needed to believe he could escape, and that nothing else would change.

"These are for you." She handed him the antique tin.

Automatically he reached out, fingers brushing hers as they closed in on the cool metal. The contrast between the cold tin and the warmth of her skin made him clear his throat again. "That's not necessary."

"I want to." Ivy leaned forward again. "You always look out for me. I've been able to build my business because you worked with me to keep the rent low. I'm grateful. I plan on expanding my menu and adding a few savory lunch items. What do you think? Would finger sandwiches be a hit?" His eyes dropped to her hands again. He almost reached out to clasp them.

Her hand flashed, fingers crossed, then not.

"A hit," he said slowly, then shook his head, remembering he was late for his game. "I have to get to the baseball field. I almost forgot. We're playing the road crew tonight."

"Tough game?"

"Well, they're a tough group of women. They usually win." He gave a wry smile.

"Shall I come watch? It might bring you luck."

"I'd love that." He could feel himself beaming. What would it be like to have this woman in the bleachers cheering him on? He might even hit a home run.

"Anyway," he scooped up the tin. They rose at the same time, and Jaxon found himself leaning toward Ivy as she leaned toward him. When she looked up, their eyes met, and time stopped. Jaxon jerked back to reality and straightened. He coughed. "I—"

Ivy shot out her hand in a businesslike gesture. "Let's shake on our agreement."

Jaxon tucked the tin under his left arm, and as he had been longing to do, took Ivy's delicate hand in his right. His hand encompassed hers. Her fingers were warm and soft, like her.

They shook. Reluctantly, he let go.

Once outside, he wanted to smack himself in the forehead. Good lord, what had he done? First, he'd leaned forward like he was moving in for a kiss. Totally inappropriate. Second, no way was he supposed to be negotiating new leases. He was leaving. It wasn't his place. But maybe, this way, her new landlord wouldn't be able to screw her over.

Right then, Jaxon determined to write up the new lease after the game. He could drop it by tomorrow. It was only decent. Jaxon prided himself on always doing the decent thing.

Derrick Cross could lump it.

Jaxon ran upstairs and changed into his uniform. His phone buzzed, and he read the text from his teammate Joel.

"Your turn for treats. Don't forget again."

"What are we, twelve?" he muttered. Now he'd need to stop at the store on his way. His eyes fell on the tin.

"Perfect." Ivy had saved him. She was good luck.

He snatched up the tin. Quickly, he put out fresh water and a dog treat for Montgomery. It was only fair since he had to stay home alone. Montgomery gave his peanut butter-flavored biscuit a delicate sniff, barked once, and gobbled it in a single swallow.

No sooner had Jaxon arrived at the game than Joel grabbed the tin. "What's this? You've gone all fancy-schmancy. A tin with a curly-girly design on it? Seriously, dude."

"It's a *fleur-de-lis*. It's French. Lay off."

"French, you say." Joel wiggled his brows and worked the lid off the tin.

"Careful, don't spill those."

Joel held the tin away from Jaxon. "Ooh, cookies? And they're pretty cookies. I know you didn't bake these." He held one up with its pressed flower design. "Dude." Joel took a bite and closed his eyes in ecstasy. He blinked at the cookie in surprise. "Wow, these are fabulous." He took another bite.

"Of course they are; they're from the tea shop. They're for after the game and for the whole team, you oaf." Jaxon made a grab for the tin, but Joel was too fast. "Quit eating them all."

"You're up to bat first, Jax. We need you to set the pace. You're our star hitter since Roman busted his ankle tripping over your dastardly dog."

"I'm the star hitter? Hardly."

"Nah, we're counting on you. Wait, you didn't bring Montgomery the Menace, did you?" Joel glanced around warily.

Jaxon frowned. "He's a tiny dog. He's not dangerous, just, you know, enthusiastic." Montgomery had been a gift he'd picked out for Candace. Montgomery had gotten him through a tough time.

"Yeah, well, he's so tiny you don't spot him underfoot until it's too late. Your dog needs to keep his enthusiasm to himself. Game's starting. You almost didn't make it." Joel gave him a shove toward home plate. "You're up."

Jaxon picked up a bat and walked to the plate. He swung it a few times to warm up before glancing at the bleachers. His breath went out in a whoosh. Ivy was there, next to her sister Holly. To her left were the four members of the Hazard Historical Society. Had everyone in town shown up to watch the game tonight? It was the Rebels, an all-male team versus the Roadies, an all-female team—the business owners versus the road crew. Everyone loved seeing the Rebels get their asses kicked by the toughest women in town.

He took a breath. Nell Coleman was pitching. That meant a fast ball, probably. Feet apart, bat ready, Jaxon braced himself. When the ball came in fast and low, Jaxon held.

"Ball."

He straightened and got in position for the next pitch. He was ready. At the curve ball flying at his head, he almost held then realized he had to swing, or it would be a strike. At the last moment he swung and missed.

"Strike," yelled the umpire, Toby, in her booming voice.

The crowd murmured. He had to do better. Joel was right. How he did would set the tone for the entire game. That was why they usually sent Roman up first. He was a real powerhouse.

Jaxon shook his head. He needed to stay focused on the ball, not the crowd. Except Ivy was in the crowd, watching. The next ball came in hard. He swung.

"Strike two!" yelled Toby.

Sweat coursed in a line down Jaxon's back. Beads of perspiration collected on his forehead. The next ball and the one after that came in high. He held.

"Ball," said the umpire.

Now Jaxon was sweating profusely. He was out of options if he planned to get a hit. With another ball, he would get a free walk to first base, or he would get a hit. He stepped back and gave a couple of practice swings. He hated the pressure of being up first. It shouldn't matter so much, but it did.

He glanced at the bleachers over to the spot where Ivy sat, leaning forward, hands clasped. Those hands, her hands—he'd touched those hands, those small, soft hands. He stepped forward and got in position. His hands choked up on the bat. The ball curved with dizzying speed. Time slowed. Everything came into sync. Ball hurtling at his head, Jaxon swung.

Bat connected to ball with a loud *thwack*.

The crowd roared. Jaxon blinked as the ball flew high. For a moment, all he could do was look on in amazement. At the peak of the arc, he heard Ivy yelling, "Run, Jaxon, run!" He heard the little laugh in her voice.

He tossed the bat and sprinted, fast, for all he was worth. He was rounding second when the fans for the opposing team groaned at a miss by their outfielder, Tessa.

The ball smacked into the mitt of the third baseman, just as Jaxon sprinted past on his way home.

*Home.*

He slid in to the sound of riotous cheers, but the only voice he could pick out was Ivy's, laughing and screaming. It was his first home run of the season.

He rose, dusted himself off a bit before he leaned over, hands on knees to catch his breath. He turned to glance at the stands. Ivy was on her feet, clapping, jumping, blonde ponytail bouncing, her sister tugging at her to sit down. He gave her a wave and headed to the dugout.

---

"Did you see that? It was amazing!" Thrilled, Ivy turned to her sister, eyes shining.

"It's the first play," said Holly, lips pinched. "We all know the Roadies will win."

Affronted, Ivy sat straighter. "They might not."

"Wanna bet?" Holly challenged.

"Yes," said Ivy. "Yes, I do."

"Confidence, dear, is very becoming," said Hazel, leaning in from her left, "but perhaps not the wisest move in this case. My money's on the Roadies. Those tough gals are total badasses."

"Goodness, Hazel, language," said Lydia, face tight in disapproval. "I'm rooting for the Rebels."

Holly raised her brow. "Ten bucks?"

"You're on." Ivy shook with her sister, cinching the deal. Holly smirked when the bottom of the first inning finished with the Roadies getting double the runs of the Rebels.

Ivy watched, cheering for Jaxon and eating her way through chili cheese nachos, a tri-tip sandwich which she shared with her sister, followed by a mini hot fudge sundae from the Community Projects ice cream cart that showed up at every game. She cheered each time Jaxon caught the ball, threw the ball, or swung a bat. It was very stressful, wanting so badly for him to win. Eating helped. Comfort food was like that. She made a mental note to add more comfort food to her new menu. As she took another bite, she could swear Jaxon could hear her cheering. His eyes always found hers when he looked toward the stands.

But the question she was dying to know the answer to

was: *Had he eaten any of the cookies?*

"Bummer, little sis," said Holly, sounding smug, when the game ended.

"Wait, what? They lost? But they were doing so well."

"Sure, until Tylene Baxter hit a homer with the bases loaded. Told you the Roadies would crush it." She gathered up all their trash. "I love making bets with you." She raised her eyebrows. "I especially can't wait until the end of this month."

"Yes, well, that is one bet you will most certainly lose," said Ivy. Beside them, money was changing hands among the Hazard Historical Society board members amidst annoyed grumbles and smug smiles. Ivy primly handed her sister a ten-dollar bill. "I'm expanding my menu."

"When did you decide this?" Holly narrowed her eyes and snatched the ten from her fingers.

"Don't squint at me like that. I'm not infringing on your turf. I'm adding *lunch* items. I went through my recipes last night, and I have some awesome ideas."

"Have you done any market research?"

Ivy mentally kicked herself. Talking business with Holly took so much effort. "Yes," she lied. "I'm starting first thing tomorrow with a soup, and a quiche du jour. You'll see. I know it'll be successful."

"Better be, to up your business by 30% by the end of the month."

Ivy grimaced when Holly couldn't see. Her and her big

mouth bragging about something she'd barely given any thought. Now she'd be up half the night, figuring out what she would make. Anxious to escape her sister before she asked more questions Ivy had absolutely no answers to, she slid out of the bleachers and ran right into Jaxon at the bottom. "Hi."

"Hi." He beamed.

"Great start to the game." She beamed back.

"Dude." Joel slapped Jaxon on the back and jerked him away. "Come on." He halted when he saw Ivy. His mouth dropped open. "Ivy." He spoke her name with reverence.

"Hi, Joel." She threw him a puzzled glance and turned to Jaxon. "Come by the shop tomorrow and try my new menu additions. I'm adding lunch items. They'll be amazing."

Jaxon hesitated. "I'd love to." Joel tugged on his sleeve. At his urgency, Jaxon shrugged and gave her a smile. "I'll be there."

Joel was nodding. "Me too." They stepped away, and he kept glancing back. She overheard him say to Jaxon, "Did she say lunch items? I'll definitely check that out."

Ivy gave a little bounce. Her plan was working—already. She knew her luck would change. She just needed to put herself out there. The world rewarded the doers, just like her aunt always told her.

Their conversation floated back at her as she started to turn way.

"Those cookies were the bomb."

"How many did you eat?"

That last was Jaxon's deep voice, the one that rumbled inside her.

"Not enough. I could've eaten a lot more."

That was Joel's tenor. Ivy had a moment of panic. Joel ate a cookie, a magic cookie? Wait, he'd said cook*ies*. Just how many of Jaxon's cookies did Joel eat?

She was about to swing back to find out when Holly grabbed her arm. "Let's go. It's starting to sprinkle." Ivy hesitated. "Unless you want to walk. Remember, you're riding with me."

With one long glance back at Joel and Jaxon, now disappearing from sight into the dugout, she took a deep breath and let her sister pull her away.

BACK AT THE dugout, Roman swung up onto his crutches from where he'd been sitting out the game and handed Jaxon the black and gold tin.

"Thanks." He frowned and weighed it in his hand. It was noticeably lighter than when Joel had snatched it off him. "Wait, did Joel leave any for anyone else? Don't tell me he ate them all."

"Nah, we all got at least one. Great treats, by the way. You should bring them to every game."

Jaxon worked the tin open. He couldn't believe it. It was

empty and wiped clean, not a single crumb remained. "Seriously, you doofuses ate them all? Ivy gave them to me."

"And you gave them to us. What did you think would happen?"

"But I didn't get any." He heard the whine in his voice. Feeling cheated, but knowing it was his own fault, he frowned. Disgruntled, he sighed and bailed on his losing team. He wasn't up to rehashing their latest defeat to the Roadies over beer and pretzels at Toby and Mac's. He had played better than ever before, but they'd still lost. At least no one could blame it on his dog this time.

He headed home to his quiet apartment. Montgomery, at least, was glad to see him. Surrounded by half-packed cardboard boxes in preparation for his move, Jaxon took his laptop to the sofa. With his dog curled beside him, he went to work on the new lease agreement for the Ivy Way Tea Shop.

# Chapter Five

IVY ADDED A tinkling silver bell to her glass door. Determined to compete with her sister, Ivy felt hers was cuter and sounded sweeter, swinging on a velvet green ribbon that matched the one on the cookie press. She'd already decided it would chime more often than her sister's, especially around midday when the bakery business was dropping off. For the first time, she would win their bet. Savory lunch items would do the trick. She'd make sure of it. Staying up late, she'd gone through her recipes and settled on tomato basil soup with little panini sandwiches of Gouda and Gruyère.

After being up half the night, she'd woken early to write her new specials in script on her whiteboard. She'd spent an hour decorating it with flowers and scrollwork. She frowned at it. The flowers resembled oleanders.

She hated oleanders. Oleanders were deadly. Sure, they were the family flowers with a long history here in Hazard, but they didn't belong in a tea shop. Tea made from oleanders would kill you. She could redraw the flowers, but who would know? The food was all prepped. Her pretty flowered teapots in all the colors of the rainbow were lined up and waiting. In addition, she had her own fresh blueberry scones today, along with Holly's chocolate croissants.

What could go wrong?

Ivy hid a yawn behind her hand as she turned her window sign from Shut to Welcome. Quiche du jour would have to wait until tomorrow. This prepping before daylight was grueling. No sooner had Ivy turned her sign than the little bell was making its happy, tinkling welcome.

"Oh!" She headed back to hold the door for Roman, who struggled with his crutches. She waited until he was clear and led him over to a table, surprised to see him in her shop. Roman was a frequent visitor at Hollister's Bakery next door. He looked incongruous seating himself at her pedestal table covered in flouncy white lace.

"What can I get you today?"

He gave her a great big grin. "I trust you. Just bring me something wonderful." He leaned in and drew in a big sniff of air. At least she hoped it was the air and not her hair. He *had* leaned in rather close.

"It smells great in here."

"I have some of the pastries from next door. Was the line too long over there for you to manage with your crutches?"

"Oh, I don't need Holly's pastries. Not today. I want something *you* baked. Do you have any cookies?" He gazed at her, eyes hopeful and adoring.

*Weird.*

"So, cookies for breakfast?" She stifled a shrug. "No problem. I'll just bring out a selection, and you can choose."

Ivy had just set about arranging a plate of madeleines, petits beurre, and her personal favorite, ginger crinkles, for Roman when the chime tinkled again.

And again.

And again.

Ivy rushed about serving her new clientele of *men*. She absolutely couldn't fathom it, all these men in her tea shop amidst the lace-curtained windows and floral-patterned china, the delicate cups and saucers. They all perched on her newly upholstered chintz-padded chairs. But the chairs *were* comfortable and the shop welcoming.

Still, it was odd to see so many male customers. The tea shop was primarily favored by a female clientele. Well, with the exception of Seymour as part of the Hazard Historical Society.

Ivy happily served tea, scones, and croissants. She made sure to hand out little slips of paper with the day's lunch offerings in the hope that she'd tempt her new customers to return midday.

Holly popped over in the midst of the rush. Her sister frowned, brow furrowed.

"What's up?" asked Ivy, as she prepared three more pots of tea and trays of goodies to carry out. "You want to give me a hand?"

"No, I don't. Where did all these men come from? Why

are they here?"

"Don't know, don't care, but I plan to keep them happy, so they'll come back." She breezed by her sister and took a tray out to Joel, second baseman for the Rebels.

"So, Ivy," he said, as she set down a blueberry scone in front of him. He took a bite and rolled his eyes in delight. "These are so, so, so good. Are you free tonight? I was hoping we could catch the play at the community center?"

"Excuse me?"

"It's a comedy, should be fun."

"Oh, I don't know, Joel. It's a little short notice for me."

"Okay, what about tomorrow, Sunday?"

"Can I let you know?"

"Absolutely, I just really want to spend time with you."

It was Ivy's turn to furrow her brow. *Why?* was her first thought. Joel had shown zero interest in her before. She'd known him since middle school. She considered her reply, and decided she might as well make a plug for her business. "Well, you could come back at lunch," she told him brightly and handed him a list of her specials.

"What's this?" said Holly, still behind Ivy's counter and glaring at the board Ivy had labored over. She waved an impatient hand at it.

"Today's lunch specials. The weather's been a bit blustery, so I thought a hot soup and sandwich combo might be popular. Say, do you have your panini maker? Mom gave us both one last Christmas. I think I could really use it today."

"Well, I'm not running home to get it."

"No, but I could probably get Aunt Lydia to get it, if you gave me the okay."

"Why would I do that?"

Ivy stopped. "Wait, are you mad?"

"Of course not," said Holly. She stood a little straighter and tugged on her pink bakery tunic. "Why would you think that?"

"Because your face is all red and you're glaring. I thought you'd be proud of me since my business picked up."

"It's *one* morning."

"The first of many." The little bell over Ivy's door tinkled. Holly stomped off.

Ivy blew out a long breath. Not her sister's best moment, which didn't seem fair. Ivy always celebrated Holly's wins.

Roman caught hold of her hand in a tight grip as she walked by. She nearly tripped as he tugged her back to his table. "Listen, I need to go man the counter at the hardware store, so my guys can unload the stock arriving in half an hour. Will you go out to dinner with me tonight?"

Ivy scrambled for a reply. "Oh, Roman, I really need to plan my menu out for the next week."

"But it's Saturday night. Please." He gave her puppy dog eyes. She gave in, and nodded. Crispy crumpets! Now Joel would find out and be mad that she'd turned him down and accepted Roman's invitation. But it was just dinner. A girl had to eat.

And Jaxon wasn't asking.

In fact, with all these men in her shop, not one of them was Jaxon. He'd said he would drop by with the new lease but had yet to make an appearance, and it was nearing ten o'clock.

Roman stood. At six foot four he towered over her, but leaned down and kissed her cheek as he worked his crutches under his arms.

"Can we keep it casual?" she asked. That would be better. Roman was definitely good-looking in his tall, dark, handsome kind of way, but she always felt too tiny next to him. She much preferred Jaxon's height. It was only an inch or two difference, but instead of feeling overwhelmed, she felt safe with Jaxon. He was the perfect height for her to tilt her head up to his. She bet she would fit perfectly in his arms.

But Jaxon hadn't asked her, and Roman had.

She'd thought she didn't want a boyfriend-type date with Roman, but maybe she actually did. She took a moment to study him. He owned the local hardware store. He was dark skinned, tall, muscular, had those deep-set brown eyes and jet-black hair. He was the regular star hitter of the Rebels, and *he* was asking *her* out.

"What did you have in mind?" asked Roman.

"How 'bout Kaylee's Refresher? It might be easier with your crutches not to have to maneuver through a restaurant with tight little tables." She bit her lip, hoping she hadn't offended him by choosing such a casual venue. Kaylee's was an outdoor burger stand, really, but super cool with high-end burgers and sandwiches that catered to every diet from carnivore to low carb to vegan to gluten free. Not to mention the rainbow selection of milkshakes.

"What's your favorite?" Roman asked, and Ivy grinned.

"Raspberry cheesecake."

"Is that a new flavor?"

"It's my new weakness."

Roman leaned in again. "Raspberry cheesecake milkshakes it is, because you, Ivy Wayland," his breath tickled her ear, and she caught hers, "are *my* new weakness."

She watched him work his way through the crowded shop to the door, deftly handling his crutches. That was kinda wow. She'd never thought of Roman as romantic. Should she consider him? Play the field? Go out on lots of dates? Would that make Jaxon notice her as a woman and not just a friend?

She shook her head, disappointed in herself. She wasn't into playing games—well, except for baking magic cookies—but apparently they hadn't had any effect on Jaxon, which meant the legend was all myth.

Of course it was. She gave herself a little shake and sighed. Magic wasn't real. Magic was illusion and artifice. Besides, she absolutely would not go out with one man to make another man jealous. That wasn't any way to treat either Jaxon or Roman. No, she would go out tonight on a casual date with Roman, so she could enjoy his company and get to know him better. She gave a decisive nod. She was a single woman who did *not* need to stay in every night of the week. She would enjoy this date on its own merits.

She would not compare Roman to Jaxon.

Much.

When Pedro from the diner across the street bustled in, Ivy hurried over to help him. She knew he must be busy. Showing up midday like this was out-of-character. Usually, it was her popping over to his diner at the end of the day to pick up takeout because she had no inclination to cook dinner for just herself after working all day in the tea shop. "What's up?"

"I wanted to pick up some of your scones for the diner."

"Oh! Oh, that's lovely." Ivy immediately began to put an order together for him.

Pedro surveyed the crowded shop, and his gaze fell on her whiteboard with the day's selections. "You've added lunch items?"

"Yes." At his perplexed frown, she added, "Oh, does that cut into your business? I didn't think about that."

Pedro laughed. "Competition is good. I've been thinking of adding Mexican specials to the menu now that my stepdad sold me his business. What do you think?"

"Oh, Pedro, that's a delightful idea. I mean, of course! Who doesn't love Leo's famous meat loaf special?" They laughed. "I know it's been a staple for…" She paused.

"Forty," said Pedro with an eye roll.

"Years," finished Ivy. They laughed again. "A cuisine a bit trendier might be in order."

"Maybe you could sample some of my ideas and let me know what you think? I have lots of ideas." He moved in a little closer. "Lots of really delicious ideas. What do you say?"

"That sounds like fun." Ivy stepped back.

Pedro stepped close again. "I know how you like fun."

Ivy turned her face up to his and blinked at him. "You do?"

"We all do." He gave a nod at the clientele pouring in the door. In that moment, Ivy suddenly realized that all her new business this morning consisted of members of Jaxon's baseball team. "I like to have fun, too. We could have fun together, don't you think?"

Ivy opened her mouth to reply and choked on her response as a disconcerting thought struck her. *Had Jaxon's entire baseball team sampled her cookies?* Was that the reason for her sudden uptick in business?

Prickles ran over her skin. She shivered at the realization that her plan to gift her Very Special Cookies had gone so far awry. That insight was followed by a wondrous recognition.

The Hazard Blessing works. *Magic is real.*

JAXON GLANCED AT the time and shut down his laptop.

He'd decided to do his business accounting from home instead of walking to his office. His stomach rumbled. Already after one p.m. meant time for lunch. Dropping in downstairs meant he could take the contract to give to Ivy.

Just the thought of seeing her midday put a spring in his step. At the shop, he paused. Her place was jam-packed. Normally, business was dropping off this time of day. She often complained her lunch business was dismal.

It didn't normally pick up until midafternoon when the bakery shut down. At the window table, Kyle and Rob, two of his teammates from last night, were having a heated discussion. That was strange—not the arguing per se, as Kyle and Rob were usually in vehement disagreement over everything—but that they would be in the tea shop at all, especially seated together. They kept glancing over their shoulders to the back of the shop. Kyle was waving his arms and Rob crossed his in dissatisfaction.

Jaxon spotted Ivy, light on her feet weaving through crowded tables, setting down plates of sandwiches and bowls of steaming soup. At the counter, pastries stacked under glass domes beckoned. His mouth watered. The sight of Ivy and pastries was inviting, but he'd been hoping for a moment when they could talk.

That was absolutely not possible with so many customers. He realized he should be happy for her, that her business was doing well. He watched while Ivy smiled and chatted as she placed down order after order. She was more enticing than the treats. He gazed, mesmerized, until he realized what he was doing. Hmm, he wasn't the only one watching her. Joel was there by the register leaning in and smiling, along with Roman, too, and Pedro.

What on earth was Pedro doing here? He had his own restaurant to run. But then Ivy was setting aside the glass dome and, with a flourish, filling an order of scones and sending him on his way.

The diner was carrying Ivy's scones now? He was pondering that when Pedro burst out the door and nearly collided with him.

"Hey, Jax, you going in?" Pedro let the door close when Jaxon glared. He shrugged, "I figured I should pick up some scones for the diner. It's the only way I can compete."

"What do you mean? Why? You have pie." *Really good pie.*

"Ah, man, no one wants pie anymore, not apple, not peach, not lemon meringue. All they want is *Ivy* and whatever *Ivy* makes."

Jaxon raised a brow.

"Her cooking, her baking, her. Ivy Wayland's all the rage. I'm losing business since the Rebels ate her cookies."

"You mean *my* cookies," Jaxon said dryly.

Pedro laughed. "Sure. Man, you missed out. Those cookies were something special." He glanced back over his shoulder. "Just like her."

"It's only been one day since you all high-graded my cookies."

Pedro kept grinning, and Jaxon was fast losing patience.

"One day, sure, and the diner was dead today, man, and not just the diner." He motioned at the bakery and a scowling Holly through her plate glass window.

Jaxon blinked. Not a single customer graced her store. Ivy's was packed. Usually, it was the other way around. Holly, as competitive as he knew she was, must be royally pissed.

"Huh." Feeling brave, Jaxon shrugged, nodded goodbye to Pedro. He stepped up to the bakery and opened the glass door. Holly's chime jingled jangled merrily. She stood straighter and brightened at his appearance. She swallowed and put on her professional smile as she smoothed a hand down her tunic.

"Good afternoon, how can I help you?"

"I just came in to—" What? See how you're taking Ivy's sudden success? He didn't know Holly well, but knew saying that would go over like a fastball in a Little League game. "To let you know there'll be some changes in the near future."

The scowl was back. "Oh?"

He nodded. "I've accepted an offer on the building."

Holly's breath came out in a whoosh. Her expression turned queasy before she smoothed it out. "This building?"

Jaxon nodded. "I want to let all my tenants know." As soon as the words left his mouth he could've kicked himself. Why was he telling Ivy's sister? She would tell Ivy and...he blinked. Ivy needed to know. He was supposed to tell her last night and instead he'd negotiated a new lease. He'd planned to tell her this afternoon. He shook his head to clear it.

"Have you told my sister?"

"*No.*" It came out more emphatically than he intended.

Holly nodded. Her eyes brightened, and her lips tilted in a smug, little smile.

At a loss as to how to extricate himself from the conversation, he perused her display case. "Can I get—" He waved his hand at a bread thingy that didn't look sweet.

"A ham and cheese croissant? I can warm it up for you."

He nodded. So much for going by Ivy's with the new lease. Not that he could've gotten in the door, let alone had a conversation with her. Instead, he took his newly warmed croissant in its pink and white striped bag to head back upstairs to eat a lonely lunch with Montgomery.

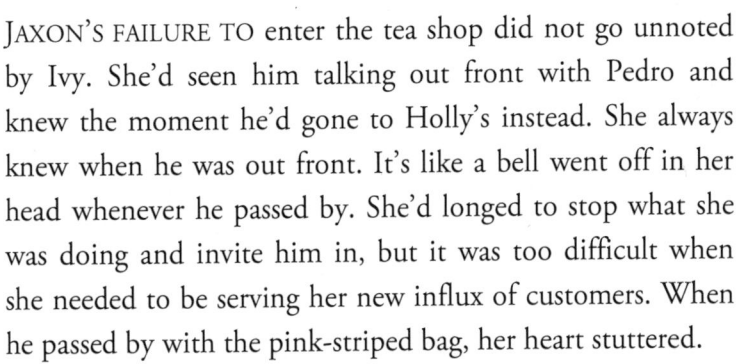

JAXON'S FAILURE TO enter the tea shop did not go unnoted by Ivy. She'd seen him talking out front with Pedro and knew the moment he'd gone to Holly's instead. She always knew when he was out front. It's like a bell went off in her head whenever he passed by. She'd longed to stop what she was doing and invite him in, but it was too difficult when she needed to be serving her new influx of customers. When he passed by with the pink-striped bag, her heart stuttered.

*Fine. Just fine.* But her stomach clenched in a knot at the betrayal. "So, Joel, thank you so much for dropping back in for lunch today. What did you think?"

"It was sooo good. I loved your tomato soup with that fancy sandwich. What do you call it?"

"Panini."

"The avocado on it was inspired."

"You think so?" Ivy had thought it inspired too. She wanted her sandwich specials to be just that. Unexpected and anything but ordinary. Encouraged by his enthusiasm, she made a quick decision. "I want to let you know that I thought about what you asked me."

Joel raised a hopeful brow. "And…" He drew the word out.

"I'd love to see the play with you. In fact, I can't wait." She gave a little jump to punctuate her pronouncement.

Joel's face split into a big grin. In response, he bounced a little on his very large feet.

Ivy grinned back. Finally, someone enthusiastic about spending time with her—well, someone besides Roman. Although he'd been pretty excited, too. And actually, she'd almost thought Pedro wanted to ask her out. Something about the way he hovered at the counter while she bagged his order. Maybe she *had* been wasting her time mooning over a grieving widower. Jaxon clearly wasn't interested and his teammates—well, they all seemed devoted to her.

All of a sudden.

Oh dear. She really needed to confirm her theory.

"Hey, Joel, quick question. Did anyone besides you eat any of the cookies I gave Jaxon for negotiating a new lease with me?"

"Is that why he had them?" Joel laughed. "That figures. He brought them to share with the team. He was on snack duty this week."

"He did?" Ivy's voice squeaked. Thunderstruck, her stomach flipped, then flopped. He'd shared them. It only confirmed her suspicion. The cookies hadn't been special to him. She had spent hours, literal hours, mixing and rolling and pressing the pattern into them. She'd baked and dealt with a freaking power failure, not to mention the slightly disconcerting high winds battering her windows over and over. She'd stayed up all night to bake him those super-special cookies. It physically hurt to learn that Jaxon gave them away.

Just like that.

Like they weren't special.

Like *she* wasn't special.

Something died a little in Ivy.

*Fine.*

She resolved to win her bet with Holly despite his non-participation. Business was already up, and she just needed to find a man who wanted a meaningful relationship with her. Her eyes wandered over the shop. Kyle and Rob stopped bickering and shook hands. What was that about?

# Chapter Six

IVY ARRIVED AT Kayley's Refresher, ready to meet Roman for their date. She'd spent an absurd amount of time trying to decide what to wear, eventually going for friendly and casual. She'd chosen blue jeans with a cute, collared, pink pastel top. She had a light rose-colored jacket in case it turned cool, and, of course, she wore open-toed shoes to show off her pale blush toenails. She'd left her hair up in her usual ponytail. She didn't want to appear too eager. It was just Roman, after all.

Ivy bit her lip, cursed her triviality. That wasn't fair to him. Roman was a great guy.

*He was.*

She straightened up, took a breath, and spotted him at a dark blue picnic table in the center of the park-like grounds.

When he looked up, she waved and wove her way through the colorful tables. The place was starting to fill up, and it was still early.

"Hey," she said. Roman stood, balancing himself with one hand on the picnic table.

He nodded and grinned. "I'll place our order. What

would you like?" He teetered a little.

"Oh, you don't need to do that. It's so far." It wasn't really, but on crutches might prove a challenge.

He laughed. "I'm buying. What would you like—well, besides a raspberry cheesecake milkshake?"

Ivy grinned. "Just a basic burger and fries—well..." She bit her lip.

"Garlic fries?"

Ivy nodded. "Yes, please. Kayley's garlic fries are the best. But only if you are too."

Roman grinned. "That can be arranged."

He took off. Even on crutches, it was clear he was athletic. It occurred to Ivy how her words might be interpreted, and she could have kicked herself. *OMG, garlic fries but only if you are too?* Now, he'd expect her to kiss him.

She scrunched her face in thought. Did she want to kiss him? She plopped down on the bench. With a head tilt, she pictured herself kissing Roman. Hmm, what would it be like? She let her imagination take off. Would it be soft or passionate? Sweet or hungry? Her heart jumped at hungry. When she thought of hungry kissing, she wasn't picturing Roman at all. Her imagination took off like a kite, soaring at the thought of hungrily kissing Jaxon, and Jaxon...was suddenly smack dab in front of her in dark jeans with a sky-blue tee, looking so delicious she could just gobble him up.

Was she hallucinating? Good lord, she was losing it.

"Hi," he said with his lopsided smile.

She blinked. He was there, really there. Like she could conjure him into existence just by wishing. "Oh, hi." He was real and right in front of her, and she felt herself break into a bright, delighted grin. Suddenly, there were loud whoops and thundering feet as the Little Leaguers rushed by, jockeying for seats at the remaining picnic tables.

One of the boys bumped into her.

"Sorry about that," Jaxon said to her and called after the boy, "Kenny, get back here and apologize."

"Oh, sorry, lady."

"Sorry, Miss Wayland," Jaxon corrected.

"Sorry, Miz Wayland," he called, racing off.

Color flooded Ivy's cheeks at her earlier thoughts. Hyperconscious at how she must appear after imagining a make-out session with the man in front of her, she knew her voice came out breathy. "You're here with the team, I take it."

Jaxon just grinned at her. After a long moment he blinked a couple of times and nodded. "Yes, they won a really tough game, so I thought a reward was in order." His expression hopeful, he added, "You could join us."

Roman chose that moment to reappear and swing his crutches up and around, barely missing smacking Jaxon in the back. He slid an arm around Ivy's shoulders. Ivy felt a definite shift in the air. Both men grew taller. Were they taking a stand?

*Over her?*

"So, Jax, looks like you've got your work cut out for you with that crowd." Roman nodded toward the Little Leaguers. "You better get over there before they get out of hand." He spoke with an edge and pulled Ivy in close, staking his claim. He leaned down and spoke softly by her ear, but loud enough for Jaxon to hear. "I got us *extra* garlic fries to share."

Roman smirked.

Jaxon's eyes widened almost imperceptibly at the blatant implication. His lips tightened before he gave a brisk nod at Roman. "You're right, I better get over to my charges." To Ivy, he gave a resigned smile.

She watched him walk away and shake his head before rounding up his team to place orders at the counter.

Roman pulled her attention back. "I arranged for Kayley to bring our order out." He put a plastic number seven on the table, and Ivy turned her focus to him. She would do this date properly.

She gave him a bright smile. "Tell me about your store."

"Really?"

"You bet. We're both business owners. I want to hear all about yours. Did you get all the inventory put away?"

Pleased, Roman launched into his day at work. It was interesting at first but somewhere amidst the details on the difference between number 45 screws and number 47 screws and the supplier mixing them up, Ivy's mind began to wander, as well as her eyes. She could see Jaxon with the boys, laughing and joking. He was great with those kids, easygoing yet firm, letting them blow off steam but keeping it all under control.

She wondered why he didn't have his own kids. He'd been married and seemed like the type. Perhaps he and his wife had run out of time. Ivy tried to concentrate on Roman, who was now talking about adding a home improvement section.

"That's a great idea," she said, and continued to picture Jaxon as a dad.

She wanted kids someday, after she achieved her other goals.

She blinked. Her goals, that's right. She was here to make them happen. Ivy settled into hearing all about front doors, back doors, screen doors, and Dutch doors.

My, but this was going to be a long date.

JAXON DIDN'T KNOW what to think. Ivy on a date with Roman? They made a handsome couple. But when did that develop? It had to be recent. Suddenly his whole baseball team was in love with his girl. The Rebels couldn't get enough of Ivy's cookies, her time, or her company.

He kept an eye on the boys busy blowing wrappers off their paper straws, aiming for each other's heads. He let out a sigh. He'd waited too long to ask Ivy out, but it shouldn't matter. He was moving to Boston, taking a job with the development company to design affordable housing.

Cookie-cutter housing.

His heart died a little at the monotony of it, but it was a means to an end. No matter that he had decidedly better ideas for affordable housing than what he was being hired for. Or that he could design more attractive units with the same budget. It wasn't what his new employers envisioned, and they'd be paying him to do exactly what they wanted.

Candace always insisted they move away from Hazard. She'd hated the town, so they'd argued, often.

Vehemently.

Now, he saw her point. The way everyone treated him like a tragedy, well, she'd been right. No way could you remake yourself in a small town. He'd struggled to persuade her to move here. Candace, ever the city girl with an adventurous streak, she'd missed the weight machines at her health club, her sports supply store, and high protein takeout. She'd urged him to move to New York, but when Jaxon balked she'd set out to convince him to relocate to Jersey City. She'd only conceded to giving Hazard a try to make their marriage work. Of course, she made it clear he owed her. An adrenaline junkie, Candace loved city life and extreme sports vacations.

All he'd wanted was stability. His childhood had consisted of a dozen different schools, as his parents forever believed the next move would be the best. It never was. One crowded apartment complex led to another, until Jaxon ached for a community where he belonged.

But how had that worked out? After Candace died, he'd moved out of the small cottage they'd rented during his marriage into an upstairs apartment in his building. Back to living in a cramped space, he'd donated all her exercise equipment to Community Projects. They'd been building a life. Now, it was all for nothing.

Still, he loved working with the Little Leaguers. Leaving would be tough. He'd planned to coach them over the years. The kids finished eating and were whooping it up again, wadding up food wrappers to launch at each other. He stood to draw their attention. Once he got them organized, he had them start calling their parents for rides.

A successful day for the team, and apparently a successful date for Roman and Ivy.

She looked fascinated by every word dropping out of Roman's big mouth. Jaxon had never thought Roman the most interesting of his friends. I mean, sure, as an architect Jaxon could appreciate hardware as much as the next guy, but Roman talking about ordering stock was a bore. But not to Ivy, or perhaps they were talking about something else. They might be making plans.

He needed to focus on his own plans. He still needed to find a neighborhood in Boston, one close to his new job, and near a park. Sighing at the number of details he still needed to work out, he put it out of his mind and thought about checking in on the sets he'd designed for the theater troupe instead. He should make sure they'd held up for opening night.

First, he needed to head home and take Montgomery for a walk. The little Scottie was supposed to have been Candace's dog, a gift she'd detested. Jaxon gave one long, lingering glance at the fresh-faced, fascinating Ivy before he waved at the last Little Leaguer getting in his parent's SUV.

A COOL BREEZE kicked up as Ivy sat listening to Roman expound on his business plans. She shrugged into her jacket, noting everyone else had left. Blue sky had dimmed to twilight. She rubbed her arms, hoping Roman would notice. At her hint, he ducked his head. "We should probably head out." She nodded, relieved the evening was coming to a close. Roman was great to look at, but not much of a conversationalist. Well, unless hardware was your thing.

She could appreciate his enthusiasm for his future, but he'd shown no interest in hers. He hadn't asked her a single question about her own business or plans. The entire evening had centered on her admiring his clever business acumen.

She waited while he got situated with his crutches on the uneven ground, and they took their time winding back to their cars. Wind tossed her ponytail, strands slipping free to spill across her eyes. Self-conscious, she sought to smooth it down.

Once at her compact car they'd stood, Roman leaning on his crutches. His eyes flicked to her wayward hair and lit up.

Oh lord, she probably radiated tousled and inviting. She hated how out of control her hair became when loose. Before she could slick her hair back down, Roman, so much taller, braced a hand to the hood of her Mazda. He angled down, just far enough for their lips to meet. Clearly, she'd been correct. The sharing of garlic fries led to expectations. Ivy hated to disappoint. Roman was a decent guy—if a bit dull—and really, it was one kiss, what was the big deal? That's how dates went, right? A meal shared, conversation, and a kiss good night.

But as Roman swooped in to make first base, Ivy froze. In the last instant, she turned her head. Soft, puffy lips brushed over her cheek in a wet smear.

Ivy cringed at the awkwardness, hoping she hadn't offended.

Roman straightened and gave her a gentle smile—rather sweet, really. She resisted the urge to wipe the wetness from his kiss off her cheek. She wouldn't be rude.

"Would you like to go out again?" He gave her a patient look as if recognizing she wasn't a girl to kiss on the first date. The yearning in his dark brown eyes almost had her saying she'd need to let him know. But a request for a second date clearly indicated he thought they were making progress. Ivy knew from her own dating experience that letting someone down "easy" and ghosting them was the worst.

She shook her head. "I enjoy your company, Roman, but..." He nodded in acceptance, truly a gentleman.

"Friends," he said.

"Friends," she agreed.

He gave her a wistful smile, and even while balancing on his crutches managed to open her car door and wait while she got in. Once she started the motor, he stepped back and gave her a wave. Ivy pulled away and paused to make sure Roman was able to maneuver to his truck and get in before she turned onto the country road back to town.

# Chapter Seven

On Sunday, business was hopping. Once again, Ivy's little tea shop was packed, and even on a day she was normally closed!

Holly was pissed.

She had come by, but not to be encouraging. That had been clear as cellophane wrap. Although to be fair, Holly had dropped off her panini maker—begrudgingly.

Today's specials were ham and cheddar panini, lavender-sage quiche, and peanut soup. The peanut soup, one of Ivy's heirloom recipes, was a hit. Who knew?

It was super tasty and different enough that everyone was on board to sample it. Ivy had apple tarts too, which she made herself instead of using the ones from the bakery. This was likely the big reason Holly was miffed. But these tarts, made from Rhode Island greening apples, were based on a recipe her mom had gifted her.

That was another reason Holly was in a tiff. She hated Ivy encroaching on *her* territory. Oh, sure, it was okay for Ivy to use pastries from Hollister's, but when it came to baking her own, she was supposed to stick to scones and cookies. Holly had lots of rules for Ivy to follow. If Ivy didn't object when Holly laid down the law, Ivy was expected to comply.

To Holly, silence was agreement. For Ivy, it had been easier to just go along.

But now? Ivy was determined to stand up for herself. She had ideas—good, sound business ideas. She could be successful. She was every bit as good as her sister.

Besides that, she had more dates than her sister.

Ivy bit back a laugh, and mentally rebuked herself for the thought, even if it was funny. And fun. She would have to share her news with the Hazard Historical Society. The community pillars were certain to be supportive.

Kyle, scarce today in the tea shop, had eagerly invited her to go to the diner and try out Pedro's new Mexican specials on Tuesday night. Rob had asked her out for an Italian dinner at the fanciest restaurant in town on Monday night.

"Miss Ivy?"

Ivy stopped at a table with young Alden Whittaker, his gaze on her both hopeful and shy, his light brown hair flopping over his forehead in youthful disarray. His dad gave the boy an encouraging nod.

"Would you come to my paintball party on Sunday, next weekend?" Big blue eyes pleaded with her to accept.

Ivy blinked at the invitation. Omigosh, how could she resist such an entreaty?

"It's my birthday."

Before she could overthink it, she said, "Sure." She couldn't disappoint a twelve-year-old. She sent a questioning glance at his dad.

"It's his mom's idea."

Ivy racked her brain to remember who Alden's mom was. Oh, that's right. Priscilla Cane, now Priscilla Whittaker. Priscilla, two years ahead of Ivy in school, had hated Ivy after Holly had beaten her out for student body president. She'd gotten back at Holly by picking on Ivy, which didn't actually bother Holly a bit. No doubt Priscilla loved the idea of Ivy getting smacked with paintballs.

But, paintball might be fun.

"I'd love to, Alden, but why are you inviting me? Are there any other grown-ups going?"

"Just you. I'm the ball boy for the Rebels, and you're the best."

Ivy had a flash of insight. "Did you try my cookies at the Rebels game?"

He nodded. "I only got one. You'll really come?"

"I will." What the heck, if Jaxon could hang out with a bunch of nine and ten-year-olds, she could hang out with a bunch of twelve and thirteen-year-old boys.

"Will there be any other girls?"

Alden bunched his lips together in an expression of distaste. "Well, my sister." He rolled his eyes. "Because Mom said she could come. All my friends like her cause she's fifteen—well"—he waved a hand near his chest—

"whatever—but I like you. Thank you. I'll see you next Sunday!"

Ivy shook her head as he dashed out the door, followed more slowly by his dad. She stacked their used dishes on a tray. The Very Special Cookies had made her popular with all ages. Could it be they really worked? It seemed so implausible, but she had lined up five dates in a little over a week. She gave an amazed laugh. No wonder Holly was ticked. Ivy was on her way to win her first bet ever against her sister.

# Chapter Eight

JAXON SETTLED INTO his seat at the back of the auditorium. One of his clients, Cece, had roped him into helping out the local community theater group, convincing him to design their sets. Set design was a new venture for him, but once he understood what they needed, he'd gotten into it. The play was a Sherlock Holmes melodrama with characters popping in and out of windows and doors. It had been a blast to design, and he'd created a four-sided version that would spin when they needed a different set for a new act.

He'd missed opening night by taking the Little Leaguers to Kayley's Refresher, so he was using his comp ticket tonight. He'd had two, but who was he going to take? Montgomery wasn't allowed in the theater. Jaxon was flipping through the program when he glanced up and saw a flash of sun-kissed ponytail halfway down the aisle.

Could it be? His heartbeat picked up. Yes, Ivy was coming down the aisle. He was about to rise and invite her to sit by him—seats weren't assigned for these small, local productions—when he saw Joel step in close and place his hand possessively on her lower back.

No way. She was on a date with Joel? Last night it was Roman, and now it was the brashest Rebel?

Jaxon endured an instant of deep betrayal and then scoffed. When had he ever told Joel he was interested in Ivy? Never, that's when. They weren't close. Besides, they were men. They didn't share feelings. He didn't have anyone to share his feelings with.

Not anymore, and kind of not even when Candace was alive.

Besides, who could blame Joel? Ivy looked—wow. She'd curled the ends of her ponytail and was dressed in a mint-green dress with a delicate white flower pattern that molded her curviness to perfection. She looked fresh, like spring personified. Joel, in an ill-fitting dark suit, was the Hades to Ivy's Persephone. Jaxon scowled. To be fair, Joel appeared mesmerized, watching her slide into her chair in a row right up front. His hand hovered right by Ivy's bottom like he wanted to cup it.

Jaxon almost rose up to rush down the aisle to stop him. But Joel halted and acted the gentleman at the last minute, sitting down beside her and handing her a program. He leaned over. Oh, were they sharing? How sweet. Heads close, they flipped through the program together.

Would they see his name? Know he had helped with the production?

He was being ridiculous. He didn't need to impress Joel, but Ivy, well—he wanted her good opinion. The auditorium began to fill. He couldn't see Ivy well, except for her honey ponytail which swam before his eyes.

Lights dimmed once, twice, and then down as Jaxon settled in to watch his set design in action.

IVY COULDN'T BELIEVE how much she was enjoying this show. It was hilarious. The characters climbing in and out of windows, and Cece's melodramatic overacting as Mrs. Hudson had her laughing until she had tears in her eyes. The whole production was a local masterpiece and whoever designed the costumes, makeup, and sets were geniuses.

How had she never come to one of these productions? When the lights swooped back up, she turned to her date with a bright smile.

"Joel, this is so much fun, thank you."

"Come on," he said, "let's hit the refreshment stand before the line gets too long." He grabbed her hand, and she let him pull her along with him up the side aisle. In line, they chatted about the play. Tea wasn't on the menu, so she ended up with a cup of black coffee and an apple crisp she recognized as her sister's. It was in a little individual sleeve with a Hollister's Bakery sticker.

She would have to see about donating some of her own scones for the next theater production. She could order new sleeves with her business name, instead of the plain white ones she used now. It'd be good advertising. Ah, maybe she was learning from her sister.

She turned and bumped into a hard body.

"Oh," she gasped. A hand raised her cup high just in time to prevent her dumping coffee all over herself.

She blinked up into brown eyes like steeped Darjeeling and lost herself for a moment in a rush of warmth. She blinked. "Jaxon, hi."

Thoughts of hungry kissing breezed through her brain. His eyes radiated hunger for just a moment. *For her?*

No, silly, he was probably just concerned she'd spill coffee all over his white shirt. He wasn't wearing a too-wide tie like Joel. No, Jaxon had no tie on at all. His bright white shirt was open at the neck and showed off tanned skin at his throat. She was suddenly fascinated by his Adam's apple. He swallowed.

Ivy blinked to clear her head, and found her voice. "Thanks for the rescue. Sorry about banging into you like that."

"My pleasure."

Jaxon's voice was a rumble deep inside her. It rippled down to her toes. She loved Jaxon's voice. It surrounded her with a sense of safety.

Joel cleared his throat, and Ivy glanced over. He was glaring at Jaxon like he wanted to squeeze that tanned throat.

Oh dear. Not again.

"So, what brought you to the play tonight?" Joel's tone

was accusing.

"Just wanted to see my hard work in action."

"What's that supposed to mean?"

"The sets. I designed them."

Ivy gave a little bounce on her toes. "Really? They're inspired. I love the way they spin for different scenes. Are there just the two sides?"

"Four. You'll see the other two in the second half."

"Can't wait. And the windows with the shades rolling up at inconvenient moments is splendid. Was that your idea?"

"It was. I read through the play several times before I started on the design."

Joel yanked on her arm. "We should get back to our seats."

Ivy hesitated. She wanted to hear more about the set design. It was so clever. "Joel, stop," she said, wrenching herself free of his grip before she could help it.

"It's okay," said Jaxon, at Joel's flash of irritation. "I won't spoil the surprise of the second half. Really, you'll love it."

"Oh, okay." She gave a little wave to Jaxon as Joel guided her away.

It took some of the fun out of the second half. She didn't know why Joel was so possessive. Roman had been the same way. And, in both cases, it was just one date.

They didn't own her.

*Men.*

Jaxon, however, had been normal. A friend.

Ugh, a friend. That was what she wanted from Joel and Roman. Just to be friends. With Jaxon, she wanted more. Her mind wandered from the show going on in front of her. She wanted to find what her parents had. She had thought, hoped, that maybe she could find that with Jaxon. If magic could be real.

Her plan had gone completely awry, but did it have to? She *could* try again. Should she make more cookies? And guarantee that only Jaxon ate them?

The set began revolving and with each inch transformed more and more into a foggy London street, with gas lights and murky corners. Ivy shivered, lost in a world of make-believe. When the set spun again for the final act, becoming a full-sized Victorian carriage in motion and jostling the passengers, Ivy clapped her hands in delight.

The end of the play had her laughing, and the kiss between Sherlock and Irene Adler had the crowd cheering, but Ivy was aware of Joel inching closer. Ivy inched away without trying to be obvious. She twisted the program in her hands. She'd enjoyed this date immensely, but was suddenly wary of it becoming awkward. She knew she had a penchant for overthinking, and that was on her.

At Joel's hand on her knee, she froze. When he squeezed and inched higher, she shot up and accidentally started a standing ovation. The crowd, applauding wildly, followed suit.

The actors on stage grinned, joined hands, and took a second bow.

As they exited and the applause died down, Joel said, "Let's go out front and greet the cast."

"Can we do that?"

"Sure, come on. They love it." He grabbed her hand, and they wound their way up the aisle with the crowd to the front steps. Half the audience milled about chatting. When the actors emerged, still in costume and full makeup, the crowd applauded.

Joel led Ivy through a receiving line so she could greet each cast member. When she got to Tessa, the Roadies's outfielder and a casual friend, she gave her a big hug and took a moment to admire her period dress up close. Tessa did a quick twirl, and Ivy couldn't help gushing. "I loved this show. I had no idea."

"Is this your first one? I'm a regular cast member now. You should come to the next one. We do four a year."

"Can't wait." Ivy gave Tessa another hug.

When Joel slid his arm around Ivy, Tessa gave her a questioning frown before the next audience member drew her attention.

Ivy lingered as long as she could, chatting with the cast while Joel rubbed her back.

The massage would have felt better if she wasn't so anxious. She liked Joel. She did. But despite the lack of chemistry, he apparently had expectations.

As the actors moved indoors and she was out of excuses to linger at the theater, Joel drew her into his side and said, "How about a nightcap at Toby and Mac's?"

"I should probably call it a night."

At Joel's nod, Ivy was relieved he didn't push, that is until he led her onto the town green away from the streetlights.

She stopped short. A walk through the dark, swaying trees in the park-like grounds made her hesitate. "Let's take a shortcut to our cars," he said, and launched into a story about his six siblings and how as kids they used to perform their own plays for his parents. When he nudged her along with him, she hated to be rude. It had really been a fabulous evening.

AFTER JAXON FINISHED checking on the set with the stage manager and tightening up some screws that had worked loose, he exited the theater to see Ivy strolling onto the green with Joel. As they vanished into the trees by the statue of Captain Edwin Hazard, Jaxon had to face the fact that Ivy was—what?

First on a date with Roman, now on a date with Joel. What was she seeking?

He had one bright, hopeful moment, then shook his head. Ivy might be ready for a guy in her life, but not a guy leaving town. He needed to face facts. The wiry, energetic

Joel had that spring in his step, as he clearly was talking Ivy's ear off. Joel could keep anyone entertained and distracted. Ivy honestly acted like she was having a great time with Joel tonight, except when he got handsy and tried to jerk her away from their conversation.

Should he follow? What if Joel didn't respect the boundaries Ivy set?

But what if nothing was wrong, and he charged after them like a lunatic? He wasn't that guy. Ivy could do what she wanted, could take care of herself. Joel wasn't some creeper. He was a local and entrenched in this town, a successful mechanic with his own repair shop, well-respected, even if he could be impetuous and pushy.

Jaxon shoved his hands in his pockets. Joel was a teammate. Ivy was her own person.

Face it, Ivy Wayland wasn't his to protect. He sucked at that anyway. He'd failed the one woman who had been his responsibility to safeguard. He hadn't saved Candace. How could he expect to do any better with someone else?

Great, he was his own nutcase with a misplaced hero complex brought on by guilt. Jaxon headed to his truck. It, too, was parked on the other side of the green, but he made himself follow the sidewalk and take the long way around.

As Ivy came abreast of the statue of Hazard's founder, Joel

spun her around to face him and surprised her with a quick buss on the lips. She was so startled at the abruptness of the move, she froze and stepped back. She felt her back press up against the base of the statue.

Joel took that as an invitation. He moved in. Ivy recognized the trajectory of his hands heading for second base. In a move she'd perfected as a teen, she stepped sideways and caught her elbow in Joel's side.

Joel stumbled a little, and Ivy took the opportunity to start walking again.

Flustered and breathing hard, she was all the way back to the sidewalk when Joel caught up.

They walked the rest of the way to their cars in silence. Joel was obviously peeved, and Ivy was mentally kicking herself for not recognizing Joel's lack of restraint earlier. She was so out of dating practice. Joel continued to walk her to her crystal-blue car. She beeped the driver door open and turned, determined to be polite. "I really enjoyed the play, thank you."

Joel scowled, but not at her. She followed his gaze. Was that Jaxon? She gave him a wave, and Joel swiveled to glower at her. "Uh, good night," she said, hopping into her Mazda, and starting the engine.

When Joel hopped in his convertible and peeled out of his parking space, tires screeching and leaving skid marks on the pavement, she leaned her head on the steering wheel. How had she managed to mess up such an ideal date?

But she knew.

She was out with the wrong man.

Jaxon strolled up beside her. She rolled down her window.

He studied her face for a moment. "You okay?"

She sought to appear composed and not flustered. "Fine. Thanks for checking." She watched Joel whipping around the corner toward Endeavor Street.

She might have said more until Jaxon gave a nod and strode off. She sat a moment watching his long strides eat up the distance toward Main. He had just done the friend thing, checking on her. She needed to accept that was all they had, all he wanted. She gripped the steering wheel, seriously considering canceling on Rob tomorrow, but that would be rude. She gave a determined sigh. She would follow through. Roman and Joel had been a bust, and Jaxon wasn't interested.

Perhaps Rob would surprise her and be the guy she could build a relationship with.

Nothing ventured, nothing gained.

Surely it would be better than sitting home amidst her herb garden, clipping bits of chamomile, mint, and rose hips to make a new tea blend. Well, except that she enjoyed creating new tea blends a whole lot more than the dating game.

# Chapter Nine

IVY USUALLY CLOSED shop every Sunday and Monday. Hollister's Bakery, of course, was open every day. Holly thrived on success, so she opened early on Sunday for faithful churchgoers to pick up their favorite fellowship doughnuts, and on Monday for office staff to bring in Danishes for their Monday morning meetings. But Ivy needed time to recharge. She only had herself to run the business. The tea shop was her labor of love. After opening up on Sunday to accommodate her many customers, she needed at least one day off. But even though her sign read closed, she spent the day transposing more family recipes and shopping for next week's supplies.

She stopped into Throckmorton Grocery for her ingredients.

Shop local. Shop Hazard.

Ivy, ever loyal, ascribed to her small-town motto even when it increased her business expenses. Holly's supplies, of course, were delivered from a large supermarket in Newport, but Ivy loved Seymour's corner market. It stocked everything she needed with quality and style.

Seymour leaned in and glanced over his shoulder before his bushy white brows drew together. He spoke conspiratorially, "How is your project working out?" His voice quavered, little more than an awed whisper.

Ivy released a soft huff. This was another reason she loved to shop here. She was understood. "Terrible. Jaxon shared his cookies with all his teammates."

Seymour puffed out his cheeks and pushed his glasses up his nose to peer down at her. "It might be what fate intended."

Ivy blinked at his unforeseen response. "What do I do about his teammates' sudden devotion?"

"Why is that a problem?"

"You saw how they all came into the tea shop. Business is booming, and I've been on two dates already, but..." Ivy shrugged, unwilling to speak ill of her lackluster dates.

"It's working." Seymour nodded, his white hair flopping with the motion.

"But Jaxon didn't eat any of the cookies."

"The Hazard blessing isn't necessarily what one expects. That's what makes it wonderful."

Priscilla Whitaker walked in, a woven, Maplewood shopping basket on her arm.

Ivy leaned closer to Seymour to keep their conversation private. "It isn't working."

He responded in a loud whisper, "Sounds to me like it's working perfectly."

Ivy leaned in closer, reluctant to be overheard by Priscilla. "But...shouldn't I bake another batch of cookies?"

"You mean those cookies Alden can't stop raving about?" said Priscilla. Ivy jumped at her caustic tone and caught her smirk as she turned to face her high school nemesis.

"Whatever you put in them has my son tripping over himself to be near you. I never would've suspected that the girl who got pantsed at the homecoming rally would be my son's first crush."

Ivy barely kept back an eye roll. It was so like Priscilla to bring that up, especially since Ivy suspected Priscilla had orchestrated the whole thing. She'd retained numerous sycophants who would've done anything to impress Hazard High's head cheerleader.

With that parting shot and a low snicker, Priscilla sashayed away toward the cake mix aisle.

Seymour shook his head, causing his white hair to wave with the motion and lowered his voice. He motioned to Ivy to move closer and, finally keeping his voice down, said, "More cookies might be dangerous. Maybe you aren't meant for Jaxon. I bet you'll find your true love with a different Rebel."

"Oh, Seymour." Ivy tossed her ponytail. "You really believe in fate?"

"You believe in magic. How is that different?" He blinked owlishly through his spectacles. "You never know what hand fate may deal. Look at me. My lady love was from a rival high school, and we had forty-four extraordinary years together, along with three children and now six grandkids. I couldn't be happier with the turn of my luck. Well, except"—Seymour got a faraway look in his eyes that hinted at cherished memories of lingering walks and laughter—"I could have enjoyed more years with my Margot."

"That's lovely."

He gave a soft sigh. "Margot helped me start these stores. Her ideas and my dedication built our dreams."

*What would that be like? A lifetime of comradery and visions realized?* Ivy pinched her lips together in thought. "So, you really don't think I should bake another batch?"

Seymour shook his head. "You could disturb the balance of the cosmos." He waved both hands in the air around his head to signify the universe. "And then what might happen?"

*I might succeed*, thought Ivy. *This time, I might get it right.*

"But don't take my opinion," Seymour added. "Check with your aunt. She knows the history of the cookie press best."

Ivy pursed her lips. "I think I'll do that." Because if anyone was likely to agree she should make a second attempt, it was Lydia LaFleur.

"Definitely not!"

Ivy jumped at her aunt's bellow. To her surprise, her

aunt was echoing exactly what Seymour had said.

She struggled to keep her cajoling tone in check. "It'll be fun. You love fun."

Lydia gave a vehement headshake. She spun abruptly and stepped into the refrigerated section of her flower shop. She glanced over her shoulder, motioned to Ivy, and pointed to an impressive container of blue hydrangeas, then at an overflowing container of pink peonies. "Choose."

Ivy pursed her lips in thought. "What's the occasion?"

"Baby shower."

"Not a gender reveal?"

"They want to be surprised."

"Oh, well, both."

Lydia grinned. "I like the way your mind works."

"So, you *do* think I should make another batch of cookies."

Lydia leaned around the tall flowers to frown at her. She waggled a free finger and almost dropped the bucket of peonies. Water splashed. Ivy dashed forward just in time to catch the peony bucket, and used her other hand to steady the hydrangeas.

"Trust in fate. Hazard knows best," said her aunt.

Ivy eased down the plastic, green bucket she was now gripping onto the counter. "Poppycock."

Lydia blinked and grabbed a paring knife. Hiding a smile, she pointed the knife at Ivy. "Stop trying to sound like me. It will not sway my opinion." She began slashing at the flower stems in a practiced motion to give them a fresh cut. "The cookies worked. Your business is on the rise. Jaxon gave your cookies away, child. Clearly, he's not interested. It must be acknowledged. The man's still in love with his dead wife."

"That's an awful thing to say." Ivy moved the waste can to catch the flying bits of slashed stems.

"Yes, it is, and I would not say it to *him*. But I *can* say it to you. Consider all your brilliant possibilities." Lydia motioned at the flowers. "You have an entire garden of men to choose from."

Ivy began to collect up items she knew her aunt would need to create the one-of-a-kind floral arrangements she was celebrated for. Ivy chose a bucket of ostrich fern and another of baby's breath, because of course you need baby's breath for a baby shower. "Is the couple married?"

Lydia shook her head.

Ivy added bachelor's button, and, for that unexpected touch, cosmos, no doubt inspired by her conversation with Seymour.

"I'm having my doubts about this said garden of men. This next Sunday is a paintball party with thirteen-year-olds."

"True, but boys grow into men."

"I'm not waiting that long," Ivy singsonged. "Remember, I have a bet to win by the end of this month."

Lydia continued as if she hadn't heard her. "And the next

generation will patronize the Ivy Way Tea Shop."

Which wouldn't be so bad. Besides, Ivy was excited to play paintball. So what if they were all kids? She was a kid at heart.

Lydia began stabbing flowers into the dampened green foam she'd placed in the bottom of a clear-cut, crystal bowl. "Tell me about your date with Roman. He's really something, that one, a real tall drink of water."

Ivy laughed and leaned on the counter to watch her aunt work. "What does that even mean? I don't think I'm all *that* thirsty."

Lydia grinned. "Tell me about the date with Joel. He's a wily one, that Joel. Doesn't he own Griffin Auto Repair? I bet he could get your motor humming right along."

"Aunt Lydia!"

"What?" She flashed her niece an innocent look. "Didn't he have something fun planned?"

"Oh, he did. We watched the melodrama at the Town Hall Theater. I adored the play. The set design was super clever." *Not to mention the set designer*, she thought, but her aunt didn't want to hear that. Ivy scrunched her lips in a pout. "But, on the dates, Roman and Joel mostly talked about themselves. Even after the play when I wanted to relive the best parts, Joel talked about his large family and the skits they put on as children."

"Of course they talked about themselves. You're a fantastic listener. That way you get to learn all about them."

"That and number 47 screws," muttered Ivy under her breath.

"What was that?" Lydia asked from behind the now towering flower arrangement.

"Nothing. Tonight I'm going out with Rob, and Tuesday with Kyle. It would be nice if just once they were interested in me and what I have to say."

"The right one will be. He'll want to know all about you. You'll find your one true love." Lydia sighed and added Ivy's selections to the arrangement. With practiced ease, she designed three large bows out of indigo, celadon, and silver ribbon.

"You sound like a fairy-tale kid's movie."

"Oh, I love those movies and you do, too." Lydia gave a decisive nod. Ivy wasn't sure if it was in approval of the flower arrangement or her statement. "Trust me, your true love is out there, and you'll find your way to him. I promise." Lydia placed the arrangement on a shelf behind her for pickup and narrowed her eyes. She waggled that long finger at her niece again. "So, do not bake another batch of magic cookies!"

# Chapter Ten

WHEN JAXON CROSSED Sawyer Bridge and spotted Hazel Bestwick at the side of the road peering under the hood of her car, he immediately pulled over. He crossed the narrow road and sauntered up behind her. "What seems to be the trouble, ma'am?" He tried to keep the laugh from his voice and failed.

She jumped and turned, then tugged her coat tighter against the cool breeze kicking up. "It's not funny, Mr. Langford. Don't think that I can't figure out what's wrong with my Lexus. I used to help my older brother with his classic Thunderbird back when I was just a girl."

"I'm positive there is nothing you cannot accomplish once you set your mind to it." He gave a nod toward the flaming-red car. "So, what's wrong?"

Hazel gave a soft harrumph. "I don't know." She pursed her lips and shook her head. "I guess it really does take a computer nowadays to diagnose car trouble."

"Let me give you a lift." He gestured toward his truck. "The sun's about to set, and you know I won't leave you alone on a country road. We can get Joel out here to tow your car to his shop tomorrow. He owes me a favor." A big one, thought Jaxon, since he'd high-graded his cookies and started taking Ivy out.

"Hmm, well, only if you take me to dinner. I was all set to enjoy a night on the town when my baby coughed and stalled."

Jaxon narrowed his eyes. "Is there really something wrong with your Lexus or are you out of gas?"

Hazel's expression was all innocent affront.

"Or are you just on the prowl to pick up a man?" Jaxon waggled his brows.

Hazel laughed out loud. "Oh dear, Mr. Langford, you are on to me, aren't you?"

With a flourish, Jaxon offered his arm. Hazel tucked hers neatly into it. He grinned down at her. "Where would milady like to go for dinner?"

"Let's go to Buonvento. I'm in the mood for Italian."

"Italian food or Italian men?"

"Both, of course. It's up the road. I wouldn't wish to put you to any trouble."

"Oh, I expect you're plenty of trouble."

At Hazel's low chuckle, Jaxon decided an evening spent with spunky Hazel Bestwick beat leftover homemade egg salad at home. Besides, one could never go wrong with the specials at Buonvento.

Ivy tried to pay attention to Rob, clad in a dark-blue suit, across the cheery, red-and-white-checkered tablecloth. He was so intense talking about his work and the importance of commercial insurance. Of course, as a business owner, Ivy had commercial insurance for the tea shop, but she didn't consider it a scintillating topic. Rob thought it was. Now, he was talking about flood insurance and how important that was.

"But isn't a hurricane an act of nature and not covered?"

He choked on his glass of merlot. She was about to stand up and come around to pat him on the back when he recovered. She glanced up just in time to see Jaxon at the hostess stand. When he took a step to the side, she could see he hadn't arrived alone, but with a woman.

*Jaxon was on a date?*

Ivy went hot and cold and her head swam a bit. Everyone swore he wasn't ready to date, that he was still mourning his sainted wife. Surely, discovering him on a date at the fanciest place in town proved he wasn't grieving.

*But who was she?*

Ivy craned, trying not to be obvious. When Rob gave her a questioning frown, she rubbed her shoulder like she was easing a crick in her neck, so he wouldn't turn to see who she was staring at. The woman, dressed in blue, was tiny, whoever she was. Was she wearing a cloche hat? With velvet trim? Too many people blocked her view for Ivy to identify her, but Jaxon looked dashing. His shirt was open at the neck, and she could see that tanned bit of skin. His sleeves rolled up not quite to the elbows, showing off forearms with a light dusting of hair, and she wondered what his arm would feel like around her, the way it was around this tiny woman. If only she could see her face.

Ivy had a flash of jealousy, imagining Jaxon holding this woman close. She racked her brain for all the tiny women in town that he might ask out and came up blank. I mean, if he liked tiny women, she kept coming back to herself. Of course, she wasn't *that* tiny, but next to him, well, they'd be perfect. She watched Jaxon until the hostess, leading him and his stylish date, went beyond where her gaze could follow.

Rob was frowning in confusion. "Where did you just go?"

"What? Oh, I was pondering what I would do in a sudden rainstorm. I've never been in a flood." She took a drink of her sparkling water. "Have you?"

Ivy was grateful the waiter arrived to enumerate the day's specials: Ziti Capricciosa and Scampi Pomodoro. She chose the ziti drowned in red sauce, topped with mushrooms and melting mozzarella. Kyle chose the scampi, which of course sounded delicious, but would make his breath fishy. She expected he'd try to kiss her at the end of their date.

She really hoped it went better with Rob. Despite her last two dates, she still felt out of practice and was certain it showed. When she glanced up from dipping her bread in balsamic and olive oil, Rob scrunched his face in puzzlement.

"Is something on your mind? You seem so far away."

"Not at all." She quickly replayed what he had been saying while her thoughts wandered. She vaguely remembered something about him working on a CPCU certification, whatever that was. "Is that difficult," she asked, "taking all those online courses? Is it like being in school?"

The lines in Rob's forehead cleared when he realized she *had* been listening, and he launched into a monologue about his many insurance certifications.

Ivy stifled a yawn.

THE HOSTESS LED Jaxon and Hazel to the back corner of the restaurant. The twenty-something hostess in her form-fitting, black lace dress had acted inconvenienced they didn't have a reservation, but really, with so few residents in Hazard one should hardly expect to wait for a table on a Monday night. The only reason for tonight's crush was a large anniversary party in the center of the room.

Jaxon held the chair out for Hazel. When he seated himself across from her, he realized he was staring at a bouncy, blonde-streaked ponytail two tables over.

Only one person in Hazard had honey-colored hair that soft and sunny, with gentle wisps falling to caress the nape of her neck. Her springy-green dress had scooped shoulders, revealing the creamy tone of her skin where the back drooped down, and, ugh, she was seated across from the Rebels's third baseman.

Another one of the cookie stealers on a date with his girl.

His mind skidded to a halt. He had no claim on Ivy Wayland. She was free to do whatever she wanted with whomever she pleased—even if it did include a date with the most tedious of all his teammates. Jaxon grabbed his water glass and took a long drink. He tore his gaze from the back of Ivy's head and focused on Hazel, now in rare form.

"I love the shadowy atmosphere here, with the soft lighting. It's very flattering, don't you think?" She ducked her head and batted her eyelashes.

Jaxon realized Hazel must once have been quite the coquette. His eyes drifted back over her shoulder to Ivy, in that mouth-watering, off-the-shoulder dress. Her soft, smooth skin made it difficult to focus anywhere else.

"These little tables are so snug and cozy. Do you get out much these days?"

Jaxon cleared his throat.

"It's time, don't you think, to get back out there?"

*Wait, was Hazel meddling? In his love life?*

She gave him guileless, wide eyes, twinkling with mischief.

Definitely meddling. Did she know Ivy would be here? Had she tipped the hostess to seat them near her table? With Hazel, it was entirely possible. Still, there were worse things in life than gazing at the back of Ivy Wayland's smooth, bare shoulders.

Just before dessert, Ivy excused herself from the table. She needed a moment. Rob was paying little attention to her as his dinner companion. Over her protests he'd ordered tiramisu to share, even though she was adamant she couldn't eat a single bite of the decadent dessert. She sighed as she made her way down the long hall past the kitchens. Perhaps she'd find a lounge where she could pause and regroup. She closed her eyes at the restful thought and collided into someone barreling out of the women's restroom.

"There you are," said Hazel, who could be cryptic on the best of days, but this was a new level, randomly showing up across town to meet with no previous arranging.

Ivy blinked. "Were you looking for me?"

Hazel gave a high-pitched laugh. "Oh, no, I've known exactly where you are all evening. The hostess seated us right behind you, just like I arranged when I called. I don't know why she acted all cranky about it. I slipped her a ten."

There was just so much to unpack in that revelation, but, concerned by Hazel's odd behavior, Ivy focused on one key point. "We?"

Hazel stood on her tiptoes, peeked over Ivy's shoulder and said, *soto voce*, "Mr. Langford and I are on a date. Marvelous, isn't it?"

Ivy blinked, and blinked again, eyelids fluttering like a hummingbird as she tried to process Hazel's words. She grasped the hands of the tiny, elderly woman in front of her. "Excuse me?"

Hazel gave Ivy's hands a reassuring squeeze. "I overheard you'd be here tonight, so I brought Jaxon. Once he fell for my car trouble ruse, I convinced him to bring me to Buonvento for dinner."

Hazel's machinations were often perplexing, but this was frosting on a nut bar. Ivy focused on Hazel's stylish hat. *She was the woman who'd entered on Jaxon's arm.* "You brought Jaxon to my date with Rob?"

"That lovely green suits you. Jaxon can't look away. Oh, I know he's trying to be polite and humor an old lady, but he only has eyes for you. You must know that."

"I don't. I—" Something eased inside Ivy. Was it true? Did Jaxon only have eyes for her? And if that was true—Ivy gripped Hazel's hands tighter. "Should I bake him another batch of cookies?"

Hazel frowned.

"I could guarantee that he's the only one who eats them."

Hazel shook her head, hat brim wobbling. "Jaxon's a generous soul. He isn't one to eat a whole batch of cookies by himself. Only a very selfish person would do that. You can't succeed by duping people, dear. The recipient must eat the cookies willingly. I fear what might happen if you rely on trickery. It breaks the spirit of the blessing. Hazard's an earnest community, defying efforts at deceit. Our founder Edwin Hazard, my ancestor, was the most upright of men."

Ivy nodded before Hazel could launch into a soliloquy on exemplary ancestry. "The cookie press came from France, though, passed through my mother's side of the family. My parents are magicians. They're absolute masters of deception."

"Well, masters *is* a bit of a stretch, don't you think?" Hazel scoffed, "That would imply your parents are good at magic. Certainly, they possess significant showmanship, but everyone knows their magic is phony. That's what makes their show so engaging. No, dear, the cookie press wasn't special when it came from France. It was only charmed after arriving in Hazard, when someone spoke the blessing over it. Before that, it was a mere cookie press—a pretty one, granted, but nothing extraordinary."

Ivy tilted her head in thought.

Hazel shook hers. "You don't need magic, dear. You need to be honest."

"But you just admitted you resorted to deception to bring Jaxon here."

"Well, yes, dear, but I'm a meddlesome old woman. No one will suspect I ran out of gas on purpose to pick Jaxon up on the side of the road. They can't conceive I'd orchestra anything so conniving." Her eyes danced, and Ivy was pretty sure no one in Hazard doubted Hazel Bestwick's propensity for deviousness. Her scheming was renowned.

"So..."

"So, do not bake another batch of your Very Special

Cookies." She looked Ivy in the eye. "Do not do it." Hazel toddled back to her table.

Ivy watched to make sure she made it. Hazel didn't seem as steady on her feet as she had even just a few weeks ago.

After taking a moment to freshen up her lipstick and mascara in the lounge's oval, gilt-edged mirror, Ivy lined her lips, hoping to make them the teeniest bit formidable. Besides, she needed to ponder Hazel's revelations about Jaxon before she headed back to Rob's less-than-dazzling conversation.

As she wound her way toward her table, Jaxon rose from his to follow Hazel toward the exit. When he came face-to-face with Ivy, his expression of wonder, followed by elation tinged with guilt made her take a step back.

"You knew I was here, didn't you? Were you going to slip out without a word?" At his astonishment, she added, "I ran into Hazel outside the restroom."

"Yes, well," he leaned down and spoke in a loud whisper like Hazel, "We're on a date."

"She told me, rather gleefully. Oh, and I doubt anything's wrong with her car that a few gallons of gasoline can't fix."

"Probably not." They smiled at each other.

"You should get back to Rob."

Ivy nodded. "I wouldn't want to miss another detailed description of covered perils."

"Or how to report a claim."

"You've spent time with Rob."

"It doesn't take long."

They grinned at each other.

"Thank you," said Ivy.

"For what?"

"For being you," she said to Jaxon's bewilderment. She returned to her table to find Rob had finished the entire dessert by himself. Well, she thought, that's one problem solved.

Rob drove her home and walked her to her door. The light was on in Holly's apartment at the end of the row, so even though her own outside light was burnt out she felt secure. Rob, his hand brushing her shoulder, eased in for a light kiss which Ivy decided might be okay until, apparently encouraged, his right hand eased around to her back and crept in the direction of third base. The nerve! Ivy adroitly sidestepped, avoiding both the kiss and the groping, to swiftly unlock her door and slip inside. "Good night," she said cheerily, "I had a lovely time." She shut the door firmly.

She leaned in, forehead on the door, until she heard his car start and then pull away.

Good lord, all the Rebels were good-looking guys, but she lacked real chemistry with any of them, except one. If it weren't for running into Jaxon, the evening would've felt like a complete waste of time.

Was she doing the right thing? Going on dates, giving these guys a chance? One might turn out to be amazing. *One of them already has,* said the voice in her head. But, for all that Jaxon always acted pleased to see her, that Hazel claimed he couldn't take his eyes off her, he'd never once asked her out.

Her breath came out in a whoosh. She would not give in to defeat. She was learning from her dates. At the theater, she learned Holly was selling baked goods at local events. If she hadn't gone out with Joel, she never would have known that.

The Hazard Historical Society's fundraiser was in less than two weeks, and her scones were every bit as good as Holly's pastries. She would guarantee her own success. Winning the bet would be fun, but improving her business remained her real goal. Nothing was going to mess that up. She'd lucked out in having her shop on Main Street, right on the square. Foot traffic was vital for a tea shop. Her business would never survive on the outskirts near Kaley's Refresher and Hopewell Nursery. People didn't drive to the edge of town for a spot of tea. So, fine, she would keep up the learning curve, and continue giving the Rebels a chance. She'd wasted too many years dreaming and watching from the sidelines.

# Chapter Eleven

Ivy plopped into the chair across from Marjorie. It was almost six p.m. and she needed to close up, but Marjorie, absorbed on her laptop, was muttering mild curse words at an Excel spreadsheet. Ivy hated to disturb her. She'd locked up at five p.m., but left Marjorie alone. Now, she needed to move her day along. She had a date with Kyle.

Ivy started pouring her latest tea blend experiment featuring Assam extra fancy with black mango and tangerine into delicate Russian teacups. For now, she was calling it Chinese Tropic. She sweetened one and set it off to the side of the laptop.

Marjorie sighed. "I'm holding you up. Thank you for letting me work late on my accounting for the tree farm."

"No problem, it gave me time to prep for tomorrow. How does chicken salad panini with pimento sound? I was able to get all the meat cooked, and I'll chill it overnight before I turn it into chicken salad in the morning."

"Delicious. What does Holly think about your new lunch items?"

"She hates them. I don't think she'll ever approve of

what I do. Her ventures are always so successful, and mine always fall short."

"I wouldn't say that. I bet she's envious she didn't create lunch specials first."

"Her bakery is so successful. If she planned to serve lunches, she'd need to put in seating."

"She has the same amount of space as you."

"True, but in the morning, the bakery's jam-packed with customers waiting their turn. She actually has them take a number."

Marjorie gave a gentle smile. "How are the goals coming?"

"I have bunches of dates. I'm meeting Kyle across the street for dinner at seven to try Pedro's new specials at the diner."

"And Jaxon?"

Ivy shrugged. She sipped her tea. Marjorie laughed.

"You aren't really being coy, are you?"

Ivy shook her head. "He went on a date with Hazel." Even to her own ears it sounded ridiculous.

"I'm sure that's Hazel's doing."

"He notices me, but never makes a move. I don't think I could be more obvious."

"Oh, you could, but I get that it isn't your style."

"Cookies are my style."

Marjorie shook her head. "You already tried that. Try something else."

"What? Short skirts and low-cut shirts? If he's taking Hazel out, that can't be his speed."

"Pshaw—you know that was just Hazel being Hazel."

"I do know that. I figure everyone must be right. He isn't ready to date. He must've loved his wife desperately."

Marjorie toyed with the edge of the tablecloth. "They were very different. As I recall, Candace liked adventure."

"I like adventure."

"Not normal adventure. Bungee-jumping adventure."

"Oh, did he go with her?"

"Once, on a rock-climbing trip which would've been tame for her but likely new to Jaxon."

"What happened?"

"Oh, that's right, you were away taking your business courses at the time. It was devastating. That was the trip when Candace fell and died."

"Oh, no." Ivy swallowed. She had heard about his wife dying, of course, but hadn't realized Jaxon had been right there with her when she fell. "How horrible."

Marjorie nodded. "Jaxon needs comfort and home. Just be you with your little tea shop. You don't need to go to extremes. I don't believe that's what he's looking for."

"I need to see this through. These dates. I have two more and then we'll see."

"No more Hazard Blessing magic. Once is enough." Marjorie sounded adamant.

Ivy tensed in defense. "My parents bake those cookies

every year and share them."

"That's different. They're in love and know what they're doing. For them, it's romantic." Marjorie slid her laptop into a black leather pouch. "Be wise, Ivy Wayland. Be wise."

Ivy unlocked the door for Marjorie. A quick gust of wind rushed inside and swirled about. It tousled her hair and made her at once wild and daring. At a rattle behind her, she turned to stare at the cookie press on the wall.

It called to her, or so she imagined. A memory teased the edges of her mind. A hint of nutmeg flitted over her tongue. She blinked. Last night, as she had drifted off to sleep, the cookie press *had* called to her.

Odd.

She shivered. A chill lingered, leaving wisps trailing through her shop like a living thing. Ivy rubbed her arms. She'd forgotten all about the dream until now. She stared at the cookie press. It had been murky, the dream. Her tea shop magically infused with mist, sparkling in moonlight. She had tried to leave because in the dream she was supposed to be somewhere, meet someone, but she couldn't find her keys to unlock the door. She would spot them, first on the counter by the register, but when she reached for them, they weren't there. Next, they were in a saucer, then on a table. She'd flitted about trying to catch them. It had been a merry chase until she'd stopped trying. Until she'd known, intuitively, where they were hiding.

She'd lifted the lid from her ivy-patterned teapot, and

with no more desire to leave, removed the keys and made a pot of tea. When the cookie press whispered to her, she'd stopped to listen. It whispered again, but she couldn't make out the words. She'd known somehow that she wouldn't be permitted to leave her shop until she baked more cookies. The press rattled, and rattled, harsher and harsher, until she'd reached for it.

Ivy reached up, her hand moving toward the cookie press, still lost in the dream. But the instant her fingers touched the cool metal, all memory of the dream flitted away like a feather in the wind.

Ivy shook her head. What happened next? The members of the Hazard Historical Society were the pillars of the community and the wisest people she knew. Every single one told her not to bake more cookies. She should heed their advice. But her fingers lingered on the press. She traced its indentations with searing fingertips.

It was just baking cookies. It couldn't go wrong every time. Not if she planned. Not if she was careful. Not if it was meant to be.

# Chapter Twelve

IVY DIDN'T BOTHER to spruce up for her date this time. The simple cotton dress she wore to work would be suitable for dinner at the diner. It was too late now to go home and change. So, she touched up her makeup. Good enough. She grabbed her little clutch purse and strolled catty-corner across the street to the diner, arriving just as Kyle, dressed in pressed jeans and a collared shirt, met her at the entrance, his timing impeccable.

Longtime waitress Dina greeted them with a raised brow. She ushered them to a booth smack dab by the front window where everyone in town could see them out together, and provided them with colorful, new menus.

As Ivy perused the menu, she was thrilled to discover Pedro had taken her advice and added Mexican entrées. She tried to ignore Kyle pulling wet wipes from a package and wiping down the entire surface of the table, along with the salt and pepper shakers and hot sauce bottles. She tried to recall if he did that when he came into the tea shop. She hoped not. She was careful to keep everything spotless. Everything was clean at the diner too, so she didn't know what Kyle's problem was.

Dina must've informed Pedro that Ivy was out front because he materialized to describe the specials. That was when everything went skidding sideways.

The instant Pedro saw Kyle with Ivy, he bristled like a paranoid hedgehog. Next, he swaggered—really, that was the only word for it—up to their booth. He rocked up on his toes and back, up on his toes and back, all the while, his deep-set eyes shooting carving knifes at Kyle.

Kyle smirked. He slid his hand across the newly wiped-down table to clasp Ivy's. His large hand encompassed hers.

Ivy gave his hand a light squeeze and tried to extricate her fingers. Kyle held on. His thumb caressed her knuckles. She tugged. He held.

She expected steam to rise off Pedro like in a cartoon, he was so hopping mad at Kyle's gesture. The madder Pedro got, the smugger Kyle grew, and the more enthusiastically he caressed her fingers.

Ivy was ready to jerk her hand free and create a scene when Pedro mumbled a curse that Ivy recognized from her high school Spanish, and began to denote the specials. His focus remained on Ivy as if they were the only two people in existence.

Every offering sounded fantastic, and Ivy got lost in his detailed descriptions. Enchiladas suizas with freshly made tomatillo salsa, carnitas tacos with pineapple-mango salsa, and beef fajitas with grilled sweet onions, green and red bell peppers, habaneros, and jalapenos.

With her attention on Pedro, Kyle's grip on her hand grew tighter and tighter.

Ivy's mouth began to water, despite the tension sparking in the air and her immediate need to extract her hand from Kyle's grasp. If the date was only about the cuisine, it would've been perfect.

As soon as Pedro finished, Kyle inserted himself. "That all sounds delicious. What would you like, sweetling?"

*Sweetling?* Ivy could've sworn Pedro grew an inch in indignation.

Before she could speak, Kyle said, "Bring all three. Let's share shall we, sweetling? That way we can enjoy *everything together*." His emphasis on the last two words only served to antagonize Pedro even more.

Just when Ivy thought Pedro would suggest he and Kyle go out back to settle the score, Pedro found his professionalism. He took a breath, gave a brisk nod at Kyle, and beamed at Ivy. "I can't wait to cook for you," he told her.

When Pedro turned, Ivy snatched her hand back. "Sweetling? Really, Kyle?"

Kyle shrugged. "You don't like sweetling? How about 'dearheart' or, I know, 'babe'?"

"Babe makes me think of Paul Bunyan's blue ox. Just stick with my name, okay? I like my name."

Kyle waved to the people passing on the street, no doubt so they would see him with Ivy. She sighed. Next the gossip grapevine would have them planning their wedding. "Sure, dearheart," Kyle said in his off-hand way, and launched into a description of his new truck. Leather seats, custom hubcaps, sunroof, whatever. Ivy could not care less. But Kyle was determined to share the great deal he gave himself on it, since he owned the Chevy dealership. Next, the conversation became a detailed description of every car in the lot and the wheeling and dealing aspects of his job.

Ivy hid a yawn while her mind scampered off on a tangent, considering dearheart as an endearment. Dearheart made her think of a hunter pulling a throbbing heart from a stag, blood dripping down, like something from a Grimms' fairy tale. Not the most romantic of images, to be sure.

Heaping platters of food arrived. Dina had to bring each one out separately, they were so overloaded. Kyle began to serve portions onto both their plates, as if he knew what Ivy preferred. It was all Ivy could do to keep Kyle from personally attempting to hand-feed her the chips and salsa, not to mention the tacos. He would make up a fajita taco adding extra salsa to it and hold it up to her mouth expecting her to take a bite. She barely resisted the urge to wrest it from his hand. He was doing it to tick Pedro off. She could feel Pedro watching them from the kitchen. She finally just focused on the enchiladas suizas. She liked those best anyway.

Dina hovered near the edge of the table, clearly enjoying the show. She could barely contain her laughter. She kept slyly winking at Ivy as if all this machismo was of great benefit.

Ivy longed to go home, but she was no quitter. She would see this date through like all the rest.

What annihilated the evening was the complimentary dessert Pedro brought to the table. A hot fudge sundae, buried in whipped cream with a cherry would have been ideal, but it arrived with a smattering of crushed walnuts. Pedro managed to fling walnut bits at Kyle when he set it down.

The glint in Pedro's eyes made it clear to Ivy that he'd done it on purpose.

Kyle hopped up, brushing madly at his clothes with the napkin. "You know I'm allergic to nuts. Why would you do this?"

Pedro responded with a Gallic shrug. "I forgot." He slid the dessert over to Ivy.

Kyle rushed off to the men's room to scrub his hands and make sure his clothes were nut-free.

When Pedro lingered at the table, Ivy waved him away with a scowl of disgust, picked up a spoon, and dived into the sundae.

She might as well.

It was forty minutes before Kyle returned. Apparently he had stripped down to check all his clothes for nut bits. Why not just go home?

Her sundae was long gone by the time he reappeared, subdued. He slumped back into the booth, rumpled and disgruntled. This date topped out as the worst yet.

Neither one spoke. What was there to say? Ivy's gaze wandered from Kyle over to Pedro putting out his "Closed" sign. Through the glass door was a view of the town green across the street. She spotted Montgomery on the end of a long leash trotting along on his little legs and where Montgomery was…

"Thank you, Kyle," Ivy said. "Sorry about the nuts." She grabbed up her clutch, shrugged into her jacket, and escaped. She brushed by Pedro on her way out without a word, because really, why? He had made an awkward date miserable beyond repair. Leaving it all behind her, Ivy made a beeline to the opposite side of the street, just in time to meet up with the only man she wanted to spend time with.

"Hey, hi," said Jaxon. He glanced at the diner, where Pedro and Kyle were obviously having words and raised an eyebrow.

"Excruciating," was all she said. He nodded. His lips gave a wry twist.

"Want to talk about it?"

Ivy shook her head. "Not ever, not for any reason. Can I walk with you?"

Montgomery was doing his delighted little doggy dance at Ivy's appearance.

"My dog says yes."

Ivy laughed. She reached down to pat Montgomery's head, and he rose on his hind legs to paw at her skirt.

When Jaxon started to scold him, Ivy held up a hand. "It's fine, really." Montgomery gave her a happy, jubilant lick, and Ivy fell into step with Jaxon. They walked a block in companionable silence. Easy. Stress-free, not like her dates with Roman or Joel or Rob or Kyle.

At the corner of Worthy and Endeavor, they paused to cross the street. Ivy sighed. "You're easy to be with."

"Nah, it's him."

Ivy gave Jaxon a bemused look.

Jaxon pointed at his dog, who scampered along. "I love taking him on walks. He's always so happy. He's the happiest little dog I think I've ever known."

"I always wanted a dog." At Jaxon's questioning glance, she added, "Holly's allergic."

"Ah."

In a moment of honest transparency into her life, she added, "So, whatever Holly needs."

"Holly gets." He nodded. "I see that. It's still like that."

Staring at the ground, Ivy shuffled her feet a little. "I didn't think anyone noticed."

"That she's a taker? I see it. You're the giver."

"So are you."

They passed Throckmorton Grocery and the one and only bar in town, Toby and Mac's. At Celestina's Chocolates, Ivy paused. She pointed. "The competition—here at the corner of Hazard and Endeavor."

"Really, I've never been inside."

"Ah, well, you're missing out."

"Nah, there's scones over there." He gave a nod toward the tea shop. "I have all I need on Main Street."

"Thank you." Ivy beamed.

They rounded the corner by the ramshackle Hazard Inn with its "For Sale" sign still out front when Jaxon shrugged. "Don't get me wrong, I like all the businesses on the square. We have everything we need right here in the center of town. I especially like that my building is part of the whole. Listen, I should really tell you…"

Suddenly, Montgomery slipped free and tore across the street. Jaxon, now holding an empty leash, muttered a curse and dashed after him in pursuit.

Montgomery barked joyfully, chasing a squirrel on the green. As the squirrel made its escape, Montgomery pawed at the base of the tree wildly. Just as Jaxon got close and leaned down to reattach the leash, Montgomery darted toward the white metal bench in the middle of the expansive lawn.

Ivy watched from the corner, not sure if she should laugh. All the other Rebels took themselves so seriously. But when Jaxon let out a loud guffaw from the green and turned back to shrug, Ivy crossed over. Jaxon waited until she caught up and angled his head toward his pet. "Dog on a mission."

The little Scottie parked his hind end by the Captain Hazard statue, waiting, as if calling them over to join him. Jaxon motioned Ivy to come along. He reached out a hand.

Ivy took it. She needed the connection after the disastrous date at the diner. Well, after all of them, really. It's like Jaxon knew she needed the human contact without expectations. Someone to understand.

That was the problem with all the dates. All the expectations they placed on her, imagining her to be what they wanted her to be and not bothering to find out what she might need. But Jaxon kept it easy, and she was certain if she were brave enough to share her thoughts, he would listen. But was that because all he wanted was a friend?

She swallowed, and it was as if Jaxon sensed her inner turmoil. He spoke, adding lightness to the moment. "I wonder if anyone ever called him Eddie."

Ivy blinked up at him and couldn't help it; she snorted a laugh. "Better than Edwin, I would think. Probably just Ed. A tough guy like him would be Ed, don't you think? I bet he had a dog, too."

"Oh? You think all the tough guys have dogs?"

*Was he flirting?*

Ivy gave him a cheeky grin. "Well, you do."

He blinked in surprise. "Yes, but he's a little dog, not a manly dog."

"Oh, I suppose manly dogs are Rottweilers and Huskies. It's not really fair to Montgomery, is it. I bet he thinks of himself as a tough, manly dog."

"He certainly doesn't lack for self-confidence."

She could hear the smile in his voice. "Hmm, how did

you come by Montgomery?" She sat on the bench with him beside her.

"He was a gift."

She turned to face him. "From?" Her eyes widened at Jaxon's pained expression. What had she said? Then it hit her. "Oh, I'm sorry." She could've kicked herself as realization flooded over her. Her voice cracked. "He was a gift from your wife." She cleared her throat. "Of course, I should have known."

Jaxon shook his head. "No." He gazed up at the sky for a long moment. "He was a gift *to* my wife…from me."

That just made it worse. Ivy's stomach took a dip and dive, but Jaxon was shaking his head.

"Don't. Please, you didn't say anything wrong. It's not…"

She held up a hand. "You don't have to talk about this."

Jaxon gave a harsh laugh. "It's not that. Really. Swear to God, Candace never even liked Montgomery."

"Really?"

"He was a terrible gift for her, a thoughtless gift. I don't think I could've given her a worse gift than Montgomery."

*How could a cute little dog be a thoughtless gift?* Ivy's heart clenched.

"I knew better, too. Candace was all about adventure." He waved his hand at the clouds. "Wingsuit flying, skydiving, white water rafting, even zorbing."

"Zorbing?"

"Don't ask." He shivered and shook his head. "If anyone thought up a crazy new extreme sport, Candace was all in. Being responsible for anyone else was *not* her idea of a good time. Having a dog meant we couldn't just pop off for the weekend. We needed to make arrangements for *that dog*, as she called him. But I—" He gave a wry smile. "I was hoping she'd change. Gifting her with a dog didn't transform her into the person I needed. It only made it clear our goals were out of alignment. She didn't even give him a name."

"What kind of woman doesn't name her dog?" The words spilled out before Ivy could pull them back. Her heart ached for Jaxon. The sky was dimming, vibrant streaks of color folding into the deep blue violet of twilight. "How long had you known each other when you married?"

"Three months. Total whirlwind, but Candace was like that. Leap first. Neither of us was what the other imagined. We had completely different expectations of what our marriage would be. We tried to make it work."

Ivy heard the grief in that statement.

"She thought I'd be into her escapades. I thought we'd build a home, at very least a home base. I knew she liked adventure, but the danger thing? That was a total surprise. We were still trying to make it work when she—fell."

Ivy swallowed hard. She didn't want to drag Jaxon through his heartache, certain it helped no one. "I should go." She rose.

"Don't."

"I hate making you relive bad memories."

"Please stay." He tugged her hand until she sat on the bench beside him. "You're helping me to make sense of my memories. No one else in town lets me talk about Candace. They're so convinced I'm miserable and grieving, but it's been three years and—" Jaxon ran a hand through his hair. It flopped down in that adorable way Ivy loved, and she experienced a flash of guilt that she could be thinking that when he was working through something so emotional.

"I'm still trying to make sense of what happened. I'd like to start over."

"Except for Montgomery."

Jaxon's mouth curved up on one edge. "Except for Montgomery. He's a keeper. I think sometimes if I'd tried harder, Candace wouldn't have died." He sighed. "It's my fault."

"Surely not."

He nodded. "We were fighting when she fell. If we hadn't been, maybe I would have been closer. Maybe she wouldn't have gone off climbing by herself. I'd have been by her side. If we hadn't been arguing, Candace wouldn't have been so reckless. If I could do it over…"

Ivy's first instinct was to soothe him, to tell him it wasn't his fault, it couldn't be, but at his wounded expression, she simply took his hand. She rubbed her fingers lightly over the back of his knuckles. "Tell me."

He released a shuddering breath. "Really?"

Jaxon needed to talk, and she could do this. This wasn't like being a good listener for her "dates" while they bragged about inventory, risk management, and fixing up a Corvette. This was being there when it mattered for someone who mattered to her.

She nodded, and was stunned at the gratitude in his eyes.

"Candace convinced me to go on her latest adventure. This one was easy, she said. One even I could handle."

Ivy took in the athletic physique of the man before her and said, in disbelief, "That even *you* could handle?"

He nodded. "Not mountain climbing, she claimed, no, no, much easier than that. It wasn't even canyoning."

"Canyoning?"

When Jaxon rolled his eyes and shrugged, they smiled at each other and said in unison, "Don't ask." His hand tightened around hers in a comfortable squeeze. "Just rock climbing, she promised, easy like those practice places kids use after school or for parties."

"Was it?"

He looked skyward. "Not even close." He laughed, and Ivy joined in.

"No, she tricked me, and it pissed me off. She thought it was hilarious and was impatient with me for being annoyed. I couldn't back out. We were already there with a group of her adrenaline-junkie buddies. I was already committed. Unless I planned to renege, my only option was to tough it out. The rock face was sheer. Oh, it wasn't high like a mountain. That much was true. We were without the climbing equipment I thought we should have. Everyone there was a veteran climber, except for me. We each had a rope and a harness. It started out fun, but the higher we got, the crazier it became. They were all extreme-sports gurus, and I was just me.

"I'm not unathletic—I played sports in high school. Even now, I'm on the baseball team with the Rebels, but this was new and not without risk. That's the part Candace loved. Taking a chance, being overconfident made her come alive. And, believe me, her confidence was staggering. It's one of the qualities I admired, but she took it too far that day. I made it to the first ridge no problem. I even made it to the second, but she kept taunting me, hinting that I'd back out.

"She wanted me to, I think, to prove I couldn't hack it, to prove we were a mistake. It made me more determined to stick it out. If everyone else could do it, so could I. By the third ridge, I'd had enough. We had space on this one. We'd moved off by ourselves, far enough from the others that no one would overhear us arguing in hushed tones. I let her have it. I told her to quit embarrassing me. That I knew she'd deceived me.

"She dared me to give up. I told her I wasn't a quitter. She lit into me about Hazard, how miserable she was and how, since I wasn't a quitter, we'd be stuck here until she died, that the reason she needed adventure was because of our pathetic life.

"We were on a ridge, halfway up a cliff. It was the absolute dumbest place to pick a fight. I'd started it, and Candace, being Candace, amped up our row until we were shouting. So much for quarreling where no one else would hear. She thrived on confrontation. Never one to back down from a fight, that was Candace.

"I chewed her out for lying to me about the skill level required, and she laughed, mocking me. All I could think was, how could she do this?

"She went off on how I was embarrassing her, that the trip was to show me what I was made of, or, rather, not made of. I said she was cruel. She said I was weak.

"I finally quit arguing. What was the point? She trudged off to check out the next section, and she left her harness behind. She rounded the outcropping—just to view the rock face, she said. But Candace always had to be first. She didn't wait for any of us to join her. Without her harness, she began to climb.

"I knew when she trudged off that I should follow. Lord, if I could do it over. That one moment haunts me. But I was angry, and at the time I thought, fine, she wants to get away from me. I'll let her."

"She was a grown woman."

"She was my wife. I should have kept her safe. It was my responsibility, but I just let her go, and then I lost her. Forever. She fell. We were all too far away to catch her, or to even break her fall. She didn't fall back to the outcropping, but all the way to the base of the rock face.

"In the last moment of her life, I wasn't there."

Ivy took his hand. "Jaxon…"

"I should have protected her."

"She—" How could she say this? She knew that Candace had been trying to escape him just as she had escaped from her dates. Candace had made her choice.

She hadn't loved Jaxon.

But had he loved her? More importantly, would Jaxon always blame himself? Because if that was the case, he might never get past his loss. *Was the town of Hazard right?* As the last bit of color faded from the horizon into darkening azure, Ivy knew she needed to go. She needed to let him go—for now.

She stepped away as Jaxon remained sitting, his loyal dog beside him. She wanted something he wasn't ready to give. At that moment, the door of the diner burst open.

# Chapter Thirteen

PEDRO SHOVED KYLE hard, yelling, "I reserve the right to refuse service to anyone, and that anyone is you!"

Arms flailing, Kyle stumbled back. He fell to one knee before he popped back up. "You're my blasted friend, and you tried to poison me. I could've died."

Pedro was shaking his head. "You always were a drama queen."

"That does it." Kyle surged forward. In lightning speed, the Rebels's pitcher drew his hand back to swing at Pedro's head. But Pedro ducked under the swing and back up, and with both hands, shoved Kyle another step back.

Kyle took a second swing. Pedro ducked and shoved. So the dance began.

Swing, duck, shove.

Swing, duck, shove…each step bringing Kyle farther away from the diner and farther into the unlit street.

"Oh, dear," said Ivy, but Jaxon was already moving. When Montgomery made a dash to go after Jaxon, she dived for his leash.

"Hey, stop." Jaxon strode into the street, as a car swerved

round the corner. Montgomery yipped and yelped as Ivy grabbed hold of his leash just in time to jerk him back from danger. Tires screeching, the car bore down. Jaxon dodged left as the car careened around Kyle and Pedro, but even that didn't give the two pause.

Swing, duck, shove.

Step by step by swing, they worked their way across the street toward the green, as the car disappeared from sight. Dina stood in the doorway, watching avidly. Ivy moved into the street and motioned at Dina to come help. Light spilled from the diner, illuminating the elderly waitress's hair to a neon shade of orange. Dina shook her head and laughed out loud.

*Really?* thought Ivy, appalled anyone would find brawling a source of amusement.

Jaxon inserted himself between the two brawlers and was ducking punches, getting hit sporadically, and dodging shoves. Kyle and Pedro continued on like he wasn't even there.

"Stop it, both of you. You're best friends."

"Friends don't serve allergic friends nuts!"

"You, idiot, I knew you wouldn't eat them. I just wanted you to leave."

"Leave? Why would I leave? I was on a date!"

"You don't deserve Ivy. She's too good for you."

"She's too good for all of us, jackass. It was my chance, and you ruined it."

Ivy bit her lip. Dear lord, they weren't fighting about the nuts at all. Two attractive, eligible men were fighting over *her*. It was surreal. Normally, she went unnoticed. How could a tin of cookies turn an entire baseball team into lovestruck morons?

Ivy knew she was nothing special, had always known that. It was her sister who was unique. Holly came in first, and Ivy always came in second.

Or last.

Jaxon got his fighting teammates separated. He stood between them, arms outstretched, holding them apart even as they reached around, still trying to hurt each other.

"Please," said Ivy, holding a barking Montgomery's leash, "if you care for me at all, go home. Just go home." The last came out on a wail, caught on the wind. Her words twined around them all.

They halted.

They stopped suddenly, like wind dying down. In eerie stillness they stepped back, away from Jaxon who dropped his arms with a long, drawn-out breath.

Pedro and Kyle shook themselves a little, still glaring at each other.

"You heard her," said Jaxon. "Get out of here." Montgomery was growling, straining against his leash now, but Ivy held on tight.

When they stepped farther back and were about four feet apart and out of punching distance, Ivy scooped up Montgomery and stepped closer into the street. The little dog shivered and twitched in her arms as she murmured and soothed him. Once he'd calmed a little, she raised her voice just enough to be heard. "Kyle, thank you. It was very thoughtful of you to take me out." Kyle gave a curt nod in acknowledgement. Before he could toss a triumphant glance at Pedro, Ivy continued. "Pedro, you are truly talented. Dinner was exceptional—well"—Ivy glanced at Kyle—"except for the nuts."

Kyle sucked in an indignant breath and turned to her, accusing, "You ate the nuts."

"I…like nuts." She gave an apologetic shrug.

"Now, I can't kiss you good night."

Everybody, even Montgomery, froze.

"I…I don't mind."

At Kyle devastated expression, Ivy could've hit her palm to her forehead. *Oh dear, how could she let him down gently.*

"Thank you both for a truly memorable evening."

Jaxon snorted a laugh, and Dina, unable to contain herself, began to applaud. Ivy flashed a warning in her direction. She was so not helping.

Jaxon started guiding Kyle and Pedro away from her. He was speaking in a low and urgent tone, but she couldn't hear what he was saying over Montgomery's yips and whines as he wiggled to be put down. Whatever Jaxon said worked, because Pedro dashed back in the diner and Kyle walked to his tricked-out car.

Once they'd cleared out, Jaxon and Ivy trailed back to the bench where her clutch lay abandoned. Contrite at being the cause of a scene, she bit her lip. "Sorry about that."

"Not *your* fault they're a couple of idiots."

She ran her fingertips over the metal scrollwork of the bench. "Idiots over me, which makes no sense."

"Oh? Makes sense to me."

Ivy blinked up at him, and he gave her that totally Jaxon smile that made her knees wobbly. "Thanks for hearing me out tonight. Let me know when I can return the favor."

"Really?" No one had made her that offer before.

"Sure, I'd love to hear whatever you have to say." He leaned in just as the darkened streetlight popped into life, spotlighting them on the green. "Although…"

Something about the half smile that flitted over his face made her ask. "What?"

"Thank you for a memorable evening?"

It took her a moment to realize he was quoting back to her what she'd said to Kyle and Pedro. She snorted and covered her mouth with her hand, and then they were both laughing hard, bending at the waist, hands on knees, as they released the tension of the past few minutes.

"You're pretty funny," he said when their laughter died down. He stepped in close and she tilted her head up.

"Oh." Ivy looked up into Darjeeling-brown eyes and lost herself a little.

Jaxon leaned in and she held her breath, anticipation

rippling through her. Was this the moment? The moment of their first kiss? Time seemed to catch its breath as well. And then, Jaxon blinked, stepped back, and gave her a wry half smile. He took the leash and she let it go, his hand brushing hers, her skin tingling from his touch.

With a brisk nod he strode away, his little dog trotting at his side.

Had he been about to kiss her? What would a kiss from Jaxon have been like?

She stared after him as he turned the corner, Montgomery scampering to keep up.

Her heart still tripping at what almost had been, Ivy waved at Dina, now locking the diner door. Ivy crossed to her own shop. She needed a moment to process the evening's events.

She flicked on the lights and set her clutch in the back. She wasn't in the mood to go back to her stark apartment. With the exception of her little windowsill garden and clothes closet, nothing in her small apartment felt like her. When she started the tea shop, she poured everything she could into it. She had brought all her special dishes and table linens to the shop. All her little decoration doodads and bits of self were here. *This* was home for her. Ivy pulled a chair down and flipped it upright. She sat. Elbows on the table and head in hands, she rubbed her eyes and took a minute to review her life.

She couldn't help mentally rehashing her disastrous date.

She had always considered Pedro a friend, yet he had clearly been annoyed she was on a date with Kyle. What was up with that? All the food he'd prepared was delicious, but if they hadn't been sharing, she had a sneaking suspicion Kyle's dinner would've been burnt to a crisp. The complimentary dessert for their table had been the epitome of mean. She hadn't realized Pedro could be that mean. But maybe it was a guy thing. Kyle and Pedro had been friends all through school. Of course, he knew about the nut allergy. They'd all known about Kyle's nut allergy. In elementary school, no one had been allowed to bring nut items to class parties. Ivy was just glad the fiasco was over, and Kyle was ok.

She needed a distraction from crazy dates. None of them cared who she really was. She was a symbol for what they craved, a vapid woman existing merely to fawn over their every word. Sure, she was a good listener, but she had ideas too. Only Jaxon valued her opinion.

Had she made a mistake baking the cookies? Jaxon had eaten none of them. She was now adored by half the male population of business owners and a teen. And, while her recent dates hadn't made her curl her toes with anticipation, she had improved her business. Had the magic of Hazard done her a favor, or was it playing a cruel joke?

Why couldn't she try again?

All the pillars had admonished her, declaring that baking more cookies was a horrendous idea, but was it, really? Another batch could provide a reset. It *had* been fun. She *did* love to bake.

Maybe she could get it right this time.

Without giving herself a chance to second-guess, Ivy rose, walked straight to the cookie press, and lifted it from the wall. "I need you," she said to it, knowing that talking to an inanimate object was irrational.

What she really needed was a reprieve from reality.

Her parents made their own reality, and they were happy. What she needed tonight was the belief that her situation would get better, that she would find true love. Just because none of her dates had been the right guy for her didn't mean they weren't ideal for someone. Roman would be great for a woman who flipped houses. Joel would be a hoot for a thespian. Kyle was perfect for a car enthusiast. Rob was perfect for—her mind went blank—a woman living in a flood zone?

Ivy took a breath to center herself and set about lovingly gathering ingredients. As calm replaced turmoil, she began to hum. She loved baking cookies. She thrived on baking these cookies.

Ivy filled her bowl with the dry ingredients and stirred, humming all the while. The tune from the last time came back to her, and she began to sing the blessing. As she warmed the butter and folded in the sugar, she pictured all the men from her dates one by one, and wished that each one would find his ideal match. Wind began to rise, buffeting the glass. A light smattering of rain joined in as an accompaniment. While she cracked the eggs, she imagined Jaxon as he'd gazed at her on the green. What would it have been like if he'd kissed her?

The raindrops grew bigger, plopping against the window as the wind blew them sideways. She loved hearing it; she found the sound comforting. Spring rains had always been a favorite. They brought new life and hope, and the ground flourished under them into green.

Vibrant green was her favorite color. Spring her favorite season. And rain on the eave above her door, her favorite sound.

Calm now, she set a kettle on to boil while she hummed. A pot of tea on a rainy night would be just the thing. Her sister preferred coffee. But that was too bitter, kind of like Holly.

She and her sister were different, yet not. They both started similar businesses. Their relationship, ever rocky, didn't diminish their solid sibling bond. She loved her sister and was certain she was loved back, despite Holly's competitive nature.

Ivy had never been a challenge to Holly before. Ivy wished they would be more congenial with each other, that Holly would take her side for once, have her back like she always had Holly's. The wind kicked up, and a blast against the windowpane made her jump and catch her breath. The sideways rain and blasting wind created a percussive, rhythmic complement. Ivy raised her voice in song. *Thou who loveth.* This storm was messier than just wind, with its big splashy raindrops, messy like her relationship with Holly. *Be blessed amongst us.* If only they could be amiable with each other. The thought expanded into a wish she'd longed for all her life. She ached for a congenial relationship with her sister. And wouldn't that be new and different? The words of the blessing tripped off her tongue. *With breath bestoweth.* Loving, blessed, not always at odds. *Thy heart.*

Ivy combined the wet and dry ingredients. She reached for the nutmeg, this time with certainty. Once the dough was in the refrigerated walk-in, Ivy studied her shop, the shared kitchen. What could she do to bless her sister?

Ivy threw herself into deep cleaning the kitchen as a favor to Holly. If she went the extra mile first, maybe Holly would reciprocate. Ivy gave a snort. Sure, that would happen. Still, if it never did, she would do this anyway.

After two hours the space was sparkling and spotless. Ivy brought out the chilled cookie dough. A storm raged now, rattling the windows. She loved how the air fair crackled with electricity. Despite being up in a ponytail, tendrils of Ivy's hair began to float free from the static in the atmosphere, reaching up toward the ceiling. She smoothed them down, but it did no good. Strands clung to her hands, refusing to be tamed. Ivy jerked her ponytail holder out and set the strands free.

The intensity in the air around her built until she tingled with it, the fine hair on her arms raised, her skin sensitive. As much as she smoothed her hair down, it still floated free.

She took a breath, rolled her shoulders, and willed herself to relax. She shoved hair away from her eyes. Static crackled. It all made sense. Change should be felt.

She washed her hands and threw a net over her hair—really, it was behaving badly tonight. She rolled out the dough and cut perfect circles in it, placing each one on a parchment-lined baking sheet. Forcing order onto the chaos, she pressed the beautiful pattern into them. Lovingly, she dusted each one with cardamom.

Letting herself feel the beat of the percussive storm, she danced her way between the counter and the oven. She baked sheet after sheet after sheet, each time placing her cookies carefully on a rack to cool.

The tea shop smelled amazing. The scent of sugar, nutmeg, and cardamom gave her a little high and she breathed in deep, drawing the scent into herself, enjoying every aspect of cookie baking. When the last cookie was set on the rack to cool, she took a moment to rest, head on her arms at the center table, and fell asleep to the sound of heavy rain.

Ivy awoke to calm. She stood and stretched, hearing her joints snap from sitting awkwardly for too long. It felt splendid. She rolled her head side to side, loosening the muscles in her neck before checking on the cookies.

Every cookie turned out perfect, flawless, enticing.

At least this time the lights had stayed on. She hadn't been in the dark about anything. Tonight had been about control—small miracle, that. She had accepted the chaos and embraced it, and the lights had stayed on. Because this time her Very Special Cookies would work.

This time, they would do exactly as she'd wished.

# Chapter Fourteen

JAXON KNEW HE needed to get on with his life. Talking with Ivy last night was wonderful, but not fair to her. He'd almost kissed her. Just because she listened. Was he so hard up for female companionship that the first sympathetic ear caused him to move in for a kiss?

Lame.

Ivy didn't know he was leaving. He'd almost told her before Montgomery flew off like a shot. He needed to be honest, but every time he tried to break the news that he was selling the building, something intervened.

He ran a hand over his face. All that would have to be sorted later because he had overslept and was late for his breakfast meeting. Derrick Cross was not a man accustomed to waiting.

Cross was key to his escape from Hazard. They'd agreed to meet at the diner before heading to the Realtor's office to finalize the details of the sale. They also had much to discuss pertaining to his new job at the Boston office. But first, breakfast.

Jaxon entered the diner to a smaller crowd than usual.

The large crowd, apparently, was across the street at the tea shop. A young waitress with dark hair and deep-set eyes, that he recognized as Pedro's sister, offered to seat him but he waved her off when he spotted Cross in a booth studying the menu. Jaxon paused. Derrick Cross looked out of place sprawled on the worn upholstery of the booth, his height and long legs ill-suited to the cramped seating. Despite his posture, his outward appearance was otherwise impeccable. Dark hair cut in an austere style, he wore a suit and radiated professionalism, even as his dark eyes flicked over the menu in decided displeasure, his lips turned down in a grimace. Jaxon slid in across from him.

Derrick put down the menu and frowned. "You're late."

Jaxon raised a brow and glanced at the clock over the counter which read eight a.m. exactly.

When the waitress hurried over, Jaxon ordered huevos rancheros while Derrick launched into a complicated order of eggs over-hard, bacon extra crispy but not charred, fresh fruit instead of potatoes, and then groused over their lack of dark rye. Jaxon chuckled at how precise and detailed Cross was over breakfast.

At Derrick's glower, he hid his laugh with a cough.

Really, if the man was this particular about breakfast, what would he be like to work for? The thought was sobering. Still, he wouldn't report directly to Derrick at the Boston firm, would he?

Jaxon shoved that concern aside for later consideration.

They were here to talk about the sale. This was a personal sale for Derrick, not part of the Boston firm business at all.

Jaxon suddenly found himself reluctant to discuss it. He wanted to talk about the job instead.

"This town." Derrick shook his head.

"Don't you like it?"

"I want to improve it. You must admit it needs help. A beautiful location with potential, but the buildings need updating."

"My building's in great condition."

"I want to buy up this entire section and would in a hot minute." He snapped his fingers. "Long past time to bring it into this century. This whole town is destined to fall into disrepair, unless someone takes a hand. That inn, for certain. I would have turned it into offices."

"Really? Instead of an inn?"

"Much better business plan. It wouldn't need as much updating. I made an offer, but was outbid. They accepted the other offer before I could counter. The new owner will need to add extra plumbing for each of the rooms. You know the old inn only had one shared bathroom on each floor. That won't work in today's hospitality market."

"I heard it was once a boarding house and before that an orphanage."

Derrick nodded. "And before that, the site of the British occupancy in the American Revolution."

"You know a lot about the history of the town."

Derrick grimaced. "The people of Hazard lack business sense. All these mansions? Like they could ever hope to compete with Newport. It's delusional. And this diner?" Derrick waved a hand. "That kitchen hasn't been updated since the 1950s."

"I don't know."

"If I owned this? I'd gut it, clean it up, and lease it to a chain. Bring in a restaurant people recognize."

"And my building?"

Derrick eyes shifted. "I'm paying market value. You'll be able to move on and be a valuable asset to the firm. We can use an architect of your experience for our development projects."

None of what Derrick said answered his question.

But should it matter? The man was right. He would move on. Hazard would be a spot in his rearview mirror. It's what he said he wanted, to leave this town behind along with the unpleasant memories of his failed marriage.

Only a month ago, he couldn't wait to shake the dust of Hazard off his feet.

Now?

"So we've decided on the price. Before the sale's finalized at the end of May, I want another look at the building. You don't mind, do you?"

"Of course not," said Jaxon, inwardly cringing at the thought of Ivy finding out this way. Why hadn't he told her before? What had he been thinking, delaying like this?

Breakfast arrived. The special was amazing; Jaxon didn't think he could have made a better choice. Derrick found fault with every bit of a breakfast that appeared fine to Jaxon. He sent his toast back as burnt, and his bacon back as undercooked. The eggs were apparently fine, but the fruit? Derrick railed at the number of grapes in it.

Jaxon held his tongue, but really it was just breakfast, a single meal. What was the big deal? It cut into their time to talk business.

After breakfast, they strolled to Jaxon's building. How would Derrick behave toward his tenants? Starting closest to the diner, they popped first into LaFleur. Today the flower shop was packed tight with product. Glass shelves shone under track lighting, inviting customers to browse for the perfect gift. China and crystal vases abounded. Two employees at the back counter busily arranged flowers, one a bouquet of a dozen pink roses and the other a complicated centerpiece of sunflowers and lilies. The refrigerated glassed-in section teemed with beautiful blooms of every color and variety. The shop smelled earthy and floral all at once, the best garden on earth.

None of it pleased Derrick Cross. Jaxon was glad Lydia wasn't there. Derrick asked what the current monthly rate was, and Jaxon told him. More frowning. Derrick inspected the front window for leaks after last night's rain, but Jaxon had installed new energy-efficient glass only the year before.

Next, they moved on to the tea shop.

Derrick frowned at the crowd in Ivy's shop. Like too much business was a bad thing? A busy tea shop meant the tenant could pay the rent.

Ivy gave Jaxon a friendly wave as she served customers. Derrick peered up at the ceiling tiles as if looking for flaws, but Jaxon knew there weren't any. He kept his property in good repair. Fortunately, they didn't stay.

Next, they stopped into the bakery, and Derrick almost relaxed upon seeing the short line. He scrutinized the floor tiles this time and Jaxon wondered why. He'd replaced them a mere six months ago. Absolutely nothing was wrong with the building. Not a single thing. Jaxon made sure of it.

It was as if the man wanted it to be falling down, seeking any excuse to raze it to the ground and start over.

But Jaxon's building was part of the charm of the square. It was older, sure, but it had character and housed a collection of successful businesses that supported the economy of Hazard.

"Tell me again your plans for the building?"

Derrick turned and exited swiftly. As they headed toward the salon, he quizzed Jaxon about the leases and any other disclosures he might want to make. It annoyed Jaxon. He'd remained totally up-front about the building, its condition, his current income from it. That was how he did business: up-front, transparent, honest.

It was why he got the job with the new architectural firm. It was what they claimed they liked about him. But his new boss, Harrison Shrift, was not like Derrick Cross, at least Jaxon hoped not. If he had to report to Derrick, he didn't think he could last long at the new firm. And selling to Derrick and then learning he'd mistreated his tenants would be an issue for Jaxon. He didn't know how he could work for someone who treated others badly.

When they left his building and crossed to the realty office on the corner of Hazard and Main, Derrick began chatting up the receptionist. He exuded fake charm and that just grated. Jaxon had liked selling his building better when he'd had no contact with the buyer. But his situation was unique. His buyer would be a new coworker at best and at worst, his boss.

# Chapter Fifteen

"Ivy, dear, would you be able to attend our next meeting for the Hazard Historical Society?"

"Wait. Why?"

Ivy's aunt Lydia was seated in the tea shop with the rest of her cronies, as usual. Her hands neatly folded on the table, hinted at an effort to appear innocent. Ivy knew all four of the pillars disapproved of her idea of baking more cookies and using the charmed cookie press, but her aunt especially had been on a mission to keep her distracted from her plan by finding inane tasks for her to complete.

First, it was cleaning the new batch of flowers that arrived late one night at the shop—after the employees had gone home. No doubt it was all orchestrated, just so she would have to help. It certainly could have waited until morning. Ivy figured it might even have cost her aunt extra to have the flowers delivered in the evening.

Next it was helping her aunt find a new dress for the Hazard Historical Society fundraiser, scheduled for Memorial Day weekend. Her aunt already owned about twenty suitable frocks. But, no, they needed to drive to Newport on

Ivy's day off. And last had been putting up flyers to find Hazel's missing cat, which at the end of the day turned out to have never been missing at all. All this to keep her distracted from baking cookies she actually had ready and waiting for the perfect moment to gift to Jaxon.

Ivy narrowed her eyes and waited for her aunt's reply. It was Hazel who answered. "We need you to take notes this month." She toyed with the bow on today's kettle brim hat and wouldn't quite meet Ivy's eyes. When Ivy waited her out, Hazel opened her own eyes wide in practiced guilelessness. "You don't mind, do you? It would be such a help."

"Notes." Ivy glanced at Marjorie, the historical society's secretary, and raised an eyebrow.

With a soft sigh, Marjorie raised her right hand, thickly bandaged. "I had an incident at the tree farm and crushed my hand under a log." At Ivy's gasp, she added quickly, "Oh, not too badly, but I won't be able to take the minutes this month. It'll be fine in a couple of weeks. Really. Don't fret."

"You don't mind, do you, dear?" Aunt Lydia spoke a bit *too* sweetly, which told Ivy they were all in cahoots. Certainly any of the others could take the notes. They didn't need a fifth wheel. They'd managed perfectly on their own for years. Although, as Ivy paused to study each one in turn, she saw that they were getting up in years. In the last three months they had started hinting about bringing some young blood into the historical society to make sure it continued on. It was a little dramatic. None of them were all so old that they couldn't do the work. All of them, except Hazel, still ran their own businesses, but Ivy supposed it was a legacy to pass onto their heirs. Ivy and Holly were included in that.

Whether or not the injury was real remained in question. Still, it probably was, as Marjorie was likely the most honest person Ivy knew.

She gave a nod. She could certainly help. "Will it be fun?"

Lydia gave her a bright smile. "So much fun. That's my girl."

"What time do you need me?"

"Six o'clock tonight. It only takes us an hour to go through the agenda."

"At the town hall on the corner?"

"Oh, no dear, we've started meeting at the mansions. Tonight, we'll be at Oleander House."

Oleander House was a stately Georgian Colonial in the south of town. "All the way out there?"

"We're working on the tours, and it's so much more inspiring to meet in the proper setting. You don't mind, do you, dear?"

"No, of course not." Oleander House had belonged to her family for more than two hundred and fifty years. Her first ancestor to arrive in Rhode Island had built it for his long-lost love in the hope that she would one day join him, but she perished in the French Revolution. So, the house was named after a poisonous bush that only sounded pretty. The house itself was magnificent, or had been in its heyday. Her ancestor eventually married a local girl. Her aunt, generations later, had grown up in the house.

Ivy had never lived in it. By the time her parents moved here with their two daughters, the mansion had been under renovation. It had remained under repair as long as Ivy had lived here, until three years ago when it was added as one of the mansions in the Hazard Historical Society's nonprofit, along with her aunt as a member. It was only recently that the historical society was able to afford the remaining renovations to restore the Georgian Colonial to its former glory.

It might be good, Ivy decided, to see its progress. She knew the new docent had begun giving tours, and she had yet to go on one, though, it sounded as though her aunt wanted to improve the script for the tours. It might be interesting to learn what she wanted to change.

At least she didn't have any dates tonight, thank goodness. She was primed to accept defeat and lose the bet. After her last dating disaster, really, cleaning up the bakery for a month sounded routine. It wasn't as if the one person she wanted to go out with would ask her.

Her eyes wandered to the glass jar where her latest batch of cookies waited. She needed the right moment to present them to Jaxon, when he was alone and might actually taste one. She glanced at the cookie press on the wall. The pillars must have noted her do it, because they immediately sought to draw her attention back to them.

"So, we'll see you tonight at six. Excellent." Lydia clapped her hands, and Ivy nodded. She left them to their plotting and returned to welcoming and serving the continual stream of customers pouring into her shop. At this rate, she might need to hire an employee.

As she was ready to clear out for the day, Holly popped in and startled her.

"Hey," she said from right beside her ear. Ivy jumped a foot in the air.

"Don't do that."

"What?" Holly was all innocence. But she knew what she did. She did it on purpose. Holly loved stomping, but since losing twenty pounds in the last year, she delighted in stepping lightly. She switched to soft shoes that made no sound whenever she wanted to be sneaky. Ivy, used to her clomping, would have to adapt.

"What's this?" Holly stared at the special glass jar of cookies Ivy was saving for Jaxon before reaching for it and drawing it in close to her body.

"Mine." Ivy reached for them, but Holly swiveled away with the jar before Ivy could grab it.

"Let's see." She tried prying the lid up, but it held tight.

"They're cookies." Ivy was about to add, *and not for you*, but that sounded churlish, like an argument they might have had as children. "I'm saving them," she said instead. Holly shrugged and frowned as she handed the glass jar back, her fingers brushing over the raised etching. She briefly gripped it tight again, before relinquishing her grasp.

Ivy took the jar carefully and refrained from blowing out a relieved breath. She didn't want to reveal how important they were. She didn't trust her sister *that* much. She loved her, yes, but Holly, as Jaxon had pointed out in their conversation on the green, was a taker. This was one thing Ivy didn't want to give. Not this time.

She set the glass jar back in its place of honor above her tea sets. The track lighting around the edge of the ceiling illuminated the etched floral design. Light reflected off the glass with a unique glow. The floral pattern swirled, almost moving on its own. Mesmerized, Ivy almost couldn't bring herself to look away. When she turned back, she saw it having a similar effect on her sister.

"I'm helping the historical society tonight." She spoke a bit too brightly to get Holly's focus off the jar.

Her sister blinked owlishly. "Don't tell me they've succeeded with you. They tried to rope me into their machinations last month. You're too easy. What do they have you doing?"

"Just taking the minutes. Marjorie hurt her hand," Ivy added quickly, "I'm not on the board."

"You're not on the board, *yet*. Be careful. They've got elections coming up. You'll find yourself with another commitment."

Ivy paused to consider. Would that be so bad? Jaxon had

lots of commitments in the community. She could put herself out there a little more. It might be good for business to be more involved in Hazard. "It's at Oleander House."

"Oh." Holly's tone held an odd note.

"What?"

Holly shook her head. "They're roping you in. You haven't seen the house since the renovations. It's spectacular. You'll love it. You will never want to leave."

Ivy scoffed.

"No, truly. No detail was spared. The wallpaper, the carpets, the furniture, the art—all authentic. The"—Holly paused dramatically, her voice just a whisper as she spoke the next word—"dishes."

"Dishes?" Ivy met her eyes.

"Dishes. Everyone knows how you delight in china patterns." Holly gave a head tilt and a shrug. "You're a goner."

"Nonsense, I have dishes. Lots of them." Ivy waved a hand at her pretty little tea sets all lined up and waiting for tomorrow's customers. "What could they have that's better than these? I've got Russian, French, Dutch, American Colonial, along with modern Lenox, Noritake, and Mikasa. I have all the dishes I could possibly need."

At Holly's knowing expression, she added, "Really? The dishes are that great?"

"You'll see."

Ivy arrived at Oleander House a good twenty minutes early. She was hoping for a chance to poke around a little before she was sucked into the Hazard Historical Society's agenda for the evening. Holly's words had sparked her curiosity. Could the dishes be as magnificent as Holly made them sound? Ivy paused to take in the stately Georgian Colonial mansion before her. Oleander House was a modest name for a structure so grand. She knew it had been built in the late 1700s after the fourth son traveled to Rhode Island from France, just a decade prior to the French Revolution. Traditionally the first son was the heir, the second conscripted for the military, and the third destined for the church. A fourth son was required to make his own way in the world. Her ancestor's timing had allowed him to keep what wealth he'd been permitted to take with him, with all the rest being lost as his family, along with his sweetheart, had been wiped out.

Ivy climbed the wide stone steps, with planters placed at intervals along the sides. Abundant blooms spilled from them all the way up to the entrance, big hydrangea blossoms in a multitude of white and pink and blue. Stunning.

She ran into Malory Stone at the door. Malory stood and waited. Hazel had it right. The thin woman's expression was grim. She stood straight and rigid, motioning Ivy in as if she owned the house. In a way, as the docent, she was the hostess.

Ivy stepped inside, and her words fled. Holly was right.

This was perfect. She paused to let the opulence seep into her. The colorful, hand-knotted carpet, true to the era, inspired thoughts of a sunrise. Framed art featured family portraits of her ancestors. She recognized the arrogant gaze of her sister and her aunt. Well, at least they came by their lofty view of the world honestly. The costuming of the figures ranged from the 1700s styles to the early 1900s.

"Come," said Malory, "the meeting will be in here." Ivy tread carefully behind the woman to the dining room, barely resisting the urge to tiptoe. Malory flipped a switch and a chandelier sprang to life, casting warm light sparkling into the corners, chasing away the shadows. A long, teakwood table gleamed, with a runner of tatted, ivory thread. A silver tray edged in gold and on it… "Oh! Oh, my." A china teapot in Famille Rose with delicate flowers hand-painted in pink and carmine had Ivy catching her breath. "Where did they find it? I thought it was lost."

Malory nodded. "From far and wide. I excel at acquisitions of this kind. The research required draws me in. We now have a complete set of twenty-four place settings," she said, clearly comfortable with touting her accomplishments.

"Twenty-four—ooh." Ivy would love to borrow a few, but Lydia would probably say no. But if she were *part* of the historical society, she might have a teeny, tiny bit of influence and could call in a favor.

She shook her head. Holly was right. The pillars were reeling her in, like a striped bass on a line.

"Have a seat. The board should arrive shortly."

"How do you like your job?"

"Honestly?" For an instant, Malory's expression transformed from grim to enraptured. Just like Ivy felt.

"It's an ideal fit, but I'm not sure the society thinks so. I'm sorry, I spoke out of turn."

"It's all right. You were a docent before?"

"No, I—well—I can bring a lot to the society. I'm a historian and well-versed in the eras of the mansions. My education includes extensive study in interior design and décor. I enjoy finding the proper pieces to furnish the mansions. Much gets lost over time. Pieces are sold, damaged, discarded. Finding the proper items to furnish the rooms to look as they did back in the day is my favorite part. Oleander House is ready for tours. We just need to finalize the script. I've made suggestions, but Lydia is quite particular. And, of course, Hazel has her own ideas, even though this isn't her mansion." Malory grimaced. "Hazel and I clash. If I don't stay on in this job, it will be due to Mrs. Bestwick."

The front door opened, and Ivy heard her aunt you-whoing. She wanted to ask Malory what she meant: if the discord between her and Hazel would lead to her deciding to move on, or if Hazel would attempt to oust her. Either was possible. For all that Hazel looked like a harmless old lady, she was a pistol and when pointed at you could be downright dangerous.

Lydia's heels clacked her way across the wood floor of the

foyer, and Malory winced. Ivy bit back a smile. Oleander House was part of the Hazard Historical Society now, but it had been Lydia's inheritance. Ivy's mother had a small interest which one day would be transferred to her and her sister, but Holly had no desire to be involved. Now that the nonprofit had been formed, it wasn't profitable in a way to suit her sister.

"Ah, there you both are. What do you think, dear? Did you get a chance to view the whole house?"

"No, not yet."

Lydia frowned disapproval at Malory, and Ivy jumped in to smooth it over. It wasn't Malory's fault that Ivy had arrived when she did. "I just got here. I'll make time to tour the house later. I promise." Ivy could see, even just from her aunt's expression, that Malory was somehow in disfavor with her employers. She couldn't imagine why. Really, who else would they find to come to the little town of Hazard to be so devoted to these mansions? The job couldn't pay well. Not for a nonprofit. It was evident from the opulence of the room that most of the funds were going into renovation and refurbishment.

Seymour arrived next, his hair in crazy disarray as if he'd braved a tornado to get in the door. Next, Hazel tottered in. For someone who could be such a force she seemed frail, so much more than usual. Malory disappeared the moment Hazel entered and reappeared with a tea tray just as Marjorie arrived, her bright red hair in pin curls that looked wind-blown as well.

Ivy paused to wonder what she had stirred up with her cookie press. It's like she had set loose the winds of change on her small community.

"Oh, my dear, I'm so glad you could make it." Marjorie waved her tightly bandaged hand for effect.

Ivy bit back a smile. "My pleasure."

Marjorie slid a binder over to her just as Ivy pulled out a laptop from her satchel. The older woman shook her head, curls bobbing. "No, no, use the binder to take the minutes."

"But wouldn't it be more efficient…" Ivy's words trailed off as they all scowled at her. Ivy threw a glance at Malory, who shrugged, as if to say, *See what I'm up against?*

The society were all seated around the table, and Malory began to pour. She apparently knew how each took their tea, which Ivy also knew of course, but she found it remarkable that Malory did as well. This must be the usual pattern of the meetings. The board sitting regally, and Malory serving. It took Ivy back in time, she supposed, to a day when the original owners would have had servants to attend them.

Malory was using the Famille Rose dishes, and it thrilled Ivy no end. Malory raised an eyebrow at Ivy as if to ask how she took her tea. Ivy blinked. "Oh, one sugar, thank you." It was so rare to be served tea by anyone other than herself. It made her feel awkward and honored at the same time. Once everyone was situated, Hazel placed her hands on the table and pushed herself up to stand. She banged her gavel smartly on the wood three times.

Malory winced visibly, her shoulders jerking with each bang of the gavel on wood.

Hazel glared at her, rolled her eyes at the rest of them, and teetered sideways before she caught herself. Ivy glanced around to see if anyone else had noticed, but no one but her seemed aware of Hazel's sudden show of weakness.

"This meeting of the Hazard Historical Society is now called to order…" Hazel's glance wandered around the room until it landed on the Georgian Mahogany Bracket Clock. She squinted. "…at 6:08 p.m."

Ivy snatched a pen from her satchel, flipped to a new page in the binder, and began to take notes.

"Old business. The nonprofit paperwork has been filed for this year. Yes?"

"Oh, yes," said Marjorie, the society's secretary. The others let out a relieved sigh. "It was quite the usual ordeal to get it all put together and submitted."

Hazel nodded. "Now, we can really move forward." She sounded pleased. "Has the search for a grant writer been successful?" She turned to Seymour, vice president.

"No," he intoned.

"Has a roofer been found for Sundial Sands?"

"No," said Lydia, treasurer.

"Has the search for an additional docent been successful?"

"No," said Marjorie.

Ivy cast a glance at Malory in time to see her shoulders twitch. Surely they didn't plan to replace her. She was doing an amazing job, and they were going to need more than a single docent for four mansions.

When the topic of the scripts came up, Malory spoke up to offer suggestions. Hazel teetered again and put a hand to her head.

Ivy jumped up and ran around the table. "Here, let me help you." She eased Hazel into the captain's chair at the head of the table. "Standing seems an unnecessary effort, and we don't mind if you sit."

"It isn't how it's done," murmured Hazel.

"You can make a change. All in favor of Hazel sitting while she conducts business say aye."

"You're not a member of the board," added Hazel.

"Aye," said everyone at the table.

"Oh, bother," said Hazel, and pounded her gavel on the table four or five times.

Malory winced again in rhythm to the pounding.

The table was hardwood. The woman could really lighten up.

"Motion passed," said Hazel, small in the upholstered captain's chair, the curved arms swallowing her up.

Lydia clapped her hands. "Yay," she said, and then stopped when no one joined in the cheering.

Seymour rose to a stand, towering over the rest of them. Ivy took her seat at the opposite side of the table while he took over the meeting.

Oh, well, thought Ivy, apparently business is done while standing. No doubt that was how it had always been done.

"On to new business," he intoned. "Let's talk about the fundraiser."

"Oh, oh, I move we hold it inside instead of in the courtyard." Lydia's eyes shone with the possibility. She clapped her hands.

"I second the motion," chirped Hazel.

Ivy glanced at Malory, who appeared queasy at the thought of so many people tromping through the newly restored mansion unsupervised.

"Discussion," said Seymour.

Ivy raised her hand and waited to be recognized. "What if you held it in the courtyard and gave tours of the inside?"

Malory relaxed perceptibly. A lively discussion ensued on the merits and problems with Ivy's suggestion. When it was determined that only the foyer, drawing room, and dining room would be open for visitors to roam free, and that the food would remain in the courtyard, Malory sent Ivy a grateful look.

Ivy raised her hand tentatively. "I have another suggestion, well—an offer. I was wondering if you would like me to provide refreshments for the fundraiser."

They stared at her.

"Holly provides refreshments for local fundraisers, dear," said her aunt.

Malory spoke up. "What would you suggest?"

"Well, scones, for one. They would be more historically accurate than, say, doughnuts."

The pillars glanced at each other, communicating silently. Marjorie made a tentative suggestion. "Perhaps if Ivy provided scones and some little savory finger sandwiches?"

Lydia picked up the idea, adding, "...while Holly provided apple turnovers and ham and cheese croissants?"

Ivy jumped in, "I could bring my special tea blend."

They all frowned. "Which one is that, dear?" asked Hazel. "Surely not My Darling Mint To Be."

"Or I Pine For You," added Marjorie, with an apologetic glance at Ivy.

Ivy didn't yet know what it would be but jumped in anyway. "I'll have teas that were locally available here in Hazard in the 1700s. I know there's a Martha Washington blend sold in Williamsburg. It'll be like that." She knew this because her mother had given it to her on her birthday. "I haven't perfected my blend yet, but I'll have it ready for the fundraiser, I promise."

Lydia clapped her hands, and the others nodded. "Excellent."

"But we won't be using the tableware inside that I've acquired," said Malory, obviously ill at the thought.

"Of course not," said Ivy to be supportive. "What will we use for serving?"

Another lively discussion ensued. It was decided a special

reception area would be set up outside. Serving platters from late in the mansion's history would display the refreshments. Guests would have clear disposable dinnerware to sample the food items. This would be classier than paper and would not put any of the items Malory had acquired at risk.

Ivy's hand was cramping by the time the meeting adjourned, but she had a better idea of what the society needed to accomplish to be successful. Really, their work was just beginning. It might not be so bad to be involved. She was excited about providing refreshments but knew Holly might not appreciate it. But really the division was fair, except for her having the tea blend, too. She needed to put substantial thought into that. She wanted a house blend for the shop. That could be the one.

Hazel and Malory had gone head-to-head over the script for Sundial Sands. Ivy had sought to smooth the disagreement but to no effect. They needed a peacemaker, but was she the right person? Someone needed to try, or they would lose Malory. The woman was a wonder, if Oleander House was any indication. Ivy couldn't wait to come back and take the tour.

She was about to leave when Malory stopped her. "I can give you a tour now. I know it's important to your aunt. I don't mind."

It wasn't that late, and Ivy didn't have anywhere to be, but surely the last thing Malory wanted to do was to give a private tour on a day she already had to work late. "You don't need to do that. I can come back at the regular time and do the tour. I don't expect you to go out of your way."

Malory deflated a little. Ivy hesitated. Where had she gone wrong? "Did you want the practice?"

The haughtiness was back. Malory gave a tight-lipped smile. "I don't need practice. I don't have any trouble memorizing the scripts."

"Oh, okay." Ivy didn't relish a private tour, and had a sudden thought. "Let's go grab a bite. I don't have anywhere to be, and I'd love to hear more about your work."

"You're humoring me. You grew up here. You must have bunches of friends to hang out with. I've heard all about how you and your sister are loved by the community and how successful you both are."

"From my aunt?"

"From all of them."

"Oh, well, Holly's the successful one. I'm just me."

"Not from what I hear."

Ivy supposed it was true, if the last couple of weeks counted. And they should, right? "I don't really have many friends here."

Haughtiness combined with skepticism reigned in Malory's gaze.

"Really, most of my friends moved away. They went off to college. Even I went to business school for a few years. But, unlike me, my friends never came back. They just moved on to bigger, busier places with fabulous career opportunities. Besides, I was never the popular one. That was my sister."

Malory still looked doubtful.

"You want to go out to Kaylee's?"

Malory arched one brow. "I thought you said you didn't have friends."

"Kaylee's Refresher. It'll be fun."

At Malory's bland expression, Ivy said, "You've never been? You've been missing out. Come with me. You'll see."

They exited together and stepped onto the front steps right into buffeting winds and drifting fog. It gave a surreal feeling to the property. Making their way down into the garden of towering oleanders, they were dwarfed by wildly waving shrubbery, wind whipping back and forth in a decidedly sinister fashion. Bits of twig caught in Ivy's hair as they dashed for her Mazda. She had never been partial to oleanders, so pretty and deadly all at once. "Ride with me. It'll be easier."

Ivy started the car, the force of the wind almost rocking it.

"This weather; I don't think I've ever lived anywhere this windy."

"So you've noticed it? Hazard was never this breezy until recently."

"Well, climate change," said Malory.

It felt like more than that to Ivy. Like she was somehow to blame, but that was hardly a thought she could share with a woman she'd just met. Once away from Oleander House the wind quit gusting, and Ivy had no trouble controlling the car.

At Kaylee's there was only a light breeze. They settled themselves at a Kelly-green picnic table on the outskirts. Malory was clearly aghast to discover the picnic seating, but Ivy didn't hold that against her. Malory was dressed in an ankle-length full-skirted dress and kitten heels. Probably not the best attire for an outdoor burger stand. But Malory made it work, and Kaylee's was an experience not to be missed. Ivy grabbed a paper menu, and Malory puzzled over it. With downturned lips, she said, "I'm not really a burger person."

"Oh, they have lots of other choices. You don't have to get a burger. But you do have to get a milkshake."

That brow raised again, and Ivy resisted squirming. Really, Malory could have been a school principal or, no, wait, a librarian. Ivy could definitely picture Malory as an old-fashioned librarian, shushing wayward talkers in the stacks. After perusing the menu, she chose a simple green salad—no wonder she was so thin—while Ivy chose a burger with everything, fries, and her favorite raspberry cheesecake milkshake.

"I'm not at all sure I want a milkshake."

"You do. You really, really do. You have to."

At Malory's clear disapproval that could rival even that of the looks the historical society gave her, Ivy added, "It's required."

"Fine, I'll go with chocolate."

That pleased Ivy. She wanted to like Malory, and you couldn't *not* like someone who went with a chocolate milkshake.

"They do it the right way? With vanilla ice cream and chocolate syrup?"

"Oh, yes, they do. Since you asked that, I know we'll be friends for sure."

Malory blinked in surprise.

Once situated with food, Ivy got Malory to share about her work. The woman adored her job, but the tours were the least of it. Malory was all about the acquisitions: following up leads on items suitable for the mansions, negotiating prices, arranging the shipping, paying to have items restored when they arrived in less than pristine condition. She thrived on overseeing the entire process. It was fascinating.

"Why are they searching for a new docent? Is it so you'll have more time to work on what you love?"

Malory scowled. "I think it's to replace me. Once the mansions are furnished, there'll be less to do."

"But won't there be more visitors? A single person can't do all the tours for all the mansions. That's crazy. The historical society will need at least one docent per mansion and a staff to clean. They'll need landscapers for the grounds. Someone will need to manage all that. The pillars have their own businesses, except for Hazel. They can't manage it all by meeting once a week, let alone once a month."

"Ha, tell them that. They think they can do it all. They have no idea of the amount of work required for their goals." Malory shook her head.

"Well, I understand."

"You're not on the board. We need someone like you."

"Like me?"

"Someone who listens. You would be great at managing a staff."

"Oh, I don't have a single employee. I'm not sure how to direct someone else's work."

"Listening is where it starts. You can't be a good manager if you don't listen."

This was a different perspective than Holly's, Ivy felt sure. "I suppose."

"And, you could manage the board."

"Do they need a manager?"

From Malory's tight lips, it was clear she thought so. She took a long sip of chocolate shake through her straw, closed her eyes, and moaned. "This is amazing. I understand now why you brought me here. These are to die for."

Ivy laughed. "My weakness."

"And now mine."

"It's good to have a friend again."

"Really?"

"Sure, don't you want to be friends?"

Malory, stone-faced, dour Malory, appeared really vulnerable for an instant. She nodded.

# Chapter Sixteen

JAXON WAS MYSTIFIED as to how he got roped into chaperoning a paintball party for a thirteen-year-old's birthday. But when Alden's dad Garrett got called into work, and Alden's mom Priscilla claimed a migraine, Jaxon got recruited to fill in. He shook his head. He could've said no, but Alden was a great kid and someone had to show up as the responsible adult or the party couldn't happen. So, paintball, really how bad could it be? A dozen middle school boys running like lunatics through the brush while brandishing paint guns—dear lord, who was he fooling?

"Okay," he said to all the faces not looking up at him. He let out a shrill whistle and raised his voice. "Pay attention. Who are the team captains?" Ronnie and Alden raised their hands high.

"Well, that means I'm on your team." Alden's pretty, fifteen-year-old sister sidled over to Ronnie. The three boys who were gathered around him cheered, then, embarrassed by their enthusiasm at a girl joining their team, shuffled their feet, eyes downcast. Jaxon, understanding the awkwardness of the age, hid a smile.

The rest of the boys divided themselves equally, and Jaxon was grateful that it happened organically and he'd avoided the choosing of teams. He counted. Perfect. So far, so good. First hurdle jumped, maybe this wouldn't be complicated. "Okay, we have an even number of players on each team."

Alden raised his voice, "But we're missing someone. I know she'll be here. She promised."

"She?"

Alden jumped up and down. He pointed down the hill. "There she is!"

Jaxon turned and couldn't believe his eyes. Ivy Wayland was strolling over the rise toward them. Hair in her signature high ponytail, she was dressed in a red, faded Community Projects sweatshirt. Black yoga pants hugged her hips, revealing lush curves. Jaxon's mouth went dry. It took a moment before he could speak. When she drew near, he asked, trying not to sound too hopeful, "Are you chaperoning, too?"

"Chaperoning?" She gave him a long perusal, and he couldn't help standing a bit straighter. "Hardly." She gave a sassy sidestep. "I'm a party guest. Right, Alden?"

"You came," Alden breathed, starstruck.

"You bet. Happy birthday. So whose team am I on?"

Shouts of "mine, mine, mine!" rang out. Jaxon wanted to chime right along with them, even though he wasn't playing.

"I guess I better stick with the birthday boy." She

stepped closer to Alden and reached out for a fist bump.

Alden regained his composure enough to complete the fist bump with Ivy before proclaiming, "That's right. You're on my team."

Ivy grinned at Jaxon.

"Hey, they have more players," wailed Ronnie. "That's not fair."

So much for uncomplicated. Before a riot broke out, Jaxon raised his arms, and said under his breath to Ivy, "Troublemaker."

"Who, me?" She batted her eyelashes.

"I'll join a team to make it even. Ronnie, I'm with you. What do you say?" The boys on Ronnie's team cheered. "Let me go get equipped. Better watch out," he told Ivy.

Ivy watched Jaxon stride down the hill to collect his own paint gun, his long legs eating up the distance. Oh, my, what had she gotten herself into? Today's confidence was all bluster. She had never in her life played paintball or even planned to. This started out as her just being nice to a boy with a crush, and now Jaxon was here? And playing for the other side? She had zip idea what she was doing. Her original plan, as she'd picked out what to wear, was to hide as much as possible. Paintballs hurt when they hit, or so Holly had gleefully told her, and bruises were not her go-to style.

She was so not the adventurous one. The fact that she considered paintball adventurous probably said more about her than she cared to admit. With Jaxon on the opposite team, she feared hiding might be challenging. She had a sneaking suspicion he might just hunt her down. Or maybe she would hunt *him* down. She found the idea of blasting Jaxon Langford with a paintball surprisingly appealing.

While the boys milled about, shoving and aiming at each other, she scoped out the grounds. Trees and shrubs provided a modicum of cover, but a tremendous amount of open space remained. How was this game played, anyway? Was it a free-for-all? Surely not, if they had teams. That, at least, meant only half the participants would be gunning for her.

She could do this.

Jaxon returned and started speaking. He looked amazing, armed with a paint gun and dressed in blue jeans and a collared tee, muscled arms bare. He'd obviously not planned to be a participant, not with how he was dressed. Despite the warm weather, Ivy had layered her clothes. Her sweatshirt hid a halter top and a long-sleeved tee. A girl needed to protect herself. She had no illusions she could escape being hit. "First off, everybody, helmets on." Jaxon waited until they'd complied.

She squinted through the helmet's opening. This made it harder. Safer sure, but she'd lost a good portion of her peripheral vision, making hiding an even more appealing plan.

"This'll be more fun with a goal." A now-helmeted Jaxon waved an orange flag. "So instead of just Last Man Standing, today's game is Capture the Flag with weapons. What do you say?"

He had such a way with these boys. More shouting and jumping by the boys commenced, followed by eye-rolling and a loud sigh from Alden's sister Rebecca. After a pointed look from Jaxon, she reluctantly slipped on her helmet.

Jaxon strode to a rise near a copse of trees and planted the flag in the round.

His voice rang out. "Team Alden, choose your base." Jaxon motioned to two other sections of trees, and Alden took off running with his teammates. Ivy followed, while Jaxon's team dashed for their base. Jaxon raised his voice to be heard by all. "Whichever team successfully grabs the flag and gets it back to their base without getting hit by a paintball is the winner. Oh, and no shooting players on their base. Okay. Game starts *now*."

Alden's team clustered round to make a plan. A plan which involved Ivy to a higher degree than she was comfortable with.

They would split into three groups. Alden really was quite the strategist. Group one would head directly for the flag. Group two would swing left, while group three swung right.

She and Alden were to slip off together to hide behind the shrubs closest to the flag. Hiding was good, but she had a sneaking suspicion she was expected to be the flag snatcher.

"You should carry the flag, Alden, you're team captain. I'll stand out too much as a girl."

He nodded. "All right."

Ivy squinted across the field to see what Ronnie's team was up to. They had completely disappeared from view.

Bad, very bad. She scanned the area. Where could they have gone?

Wait. Ivy spotted Rebecca.

Splat.

"Ugh," shouted Rebecca. She whipped off her helmet and threw it on the ground, where it bounced a couple of times. "Look at me!" With both hands, she pointed at the big red splat on her white sweatshirt. "I knew this would suck." She stomped off, kicking the helmet just as another splat hit the boy who'd shot Rebecca.

"Wait, Becca, wait up. I'll keep you company." Scooping up her helmet, the boy chased after her, sounding not at all bummed to hang out with the buxom Becca.

Ivy glanced behind her. *Where was the shooter?* Then, she spied him. A member of Ronnie's team was tucked high up in the Y of a tree, concealed by leaves. Ah, so they had a sniper. Clever. She wished she'd thought of it. No doubt Jaxon was responsible for that bit of brilliance.

They'd need to up their game. Ivy slipped down the hill and away, sneaking and keeping her head low to stay out of sight. Her goal was to stay "alive" as long as possible. She wasn't really into shooting any of the boys. Nope, she was gunning for Jaxon. Hitting Jaxon in the ass had become her number one goal. Alden was sneaking alongside. "Where are you going?" he whispered.

"To take out Jaxon."

"We need to get the flag."

"But Jaxon's giving Ronnie great ideas. I bet he thought up that sniper-in-the-tree bit."

"Sure, but they should've synchronized their attacks. Now we're scanning the trees. See, right there." He pointed up to another boy stretched out horizontally, high up in a white oak about eight feet away. Alden motioned to her to crawl through the shrubs. "With me." When she nodded, they belly-crept along the ground until they were just below the tree. The boy had taken aim at a camo-clad member of Team Alden dashing through the clearing.

In hushed tones so soft Ivy had to strain to hear, Alden said, "Ready. Aim. Fire."

Ivy and Alden fired in quick succession. The tree-bound sniper avoided Ivy's attempt, but in doing so, swung right into the paintball fired by Alden. "Yes!" Alden gave a fist pump. "See, we make a great team."

Ivy grinned. The sniper swung down, gave a sheepish wave at Alden, and sprinted off to seek out Rebecca. Hanging with Alden's sister was serving as a consolation prize for everyone out of the game.

Ivy glimpsed Jaxon running low, head down, toward a group of boys to give instructions. This was her chance. If she could just…

Alden's grip on her arm stopped her. He shook his head.

"Don't give away our position. There's too many of them."

He was right. Getting Jaxon would be fun, but it would sacrifice them, and Alden deserved to play until the end. Ivy decided in that moment to make sure Alden remained the last man standing. She was covered in brambles now, and uncomfortable, but it was a small price to pay to give Alden a memorable birthday.

She listened to Jaxon giving orders.

"Okay, Antony, you and Edgar, you're on flag duty. Not to grab but to guard. Rex, you and Preston will keep the snipers safe. We don't want to lose any more snipers. Cody and Nathan, you two stick to the sidelines and pick off whoever you can."

"What about Ivy and Alden? No one has seen them. Ivy's a girl. I bet I could pick her off easy."

"No," Jaxon said, "Ivy is mine."

A chill of anticipation traveled from the tip of Ivy's head along her spine to her toes at Jaxon's vow.

*She was his?* Oh-ho, no, he was hers. Now she was even more determined to take him out, but she'd stay true to her primary objective: keep Alden free of paintballs. Make this his best birthday ever.

Getting Jaxon—oh yeah, she'd do that, too.

Alden was tugging on her sleeve whispering instructions. She'd have to leave Jaxon for later. Right now, she was Alden's bodyguard.

Jaxon knew Ivy was out there. He could sense her. It was almost like he knew she was watching him, but that was ridiculous. Surely just his imagination. Or him hoping. He spent a lot of time wondering about Ivy and worrying how his decisions would affect her. His choices might impact her whole life, not in paintball, but in selling the building. He shook his head. He needed to keep his head in the game. Right now his goal needed to be giving these kids a fun time at paintball.

All other concerns needed to wait. But taking out his number one sniper had been inspired. He'd seen Ivy with Alden in that double-pronged attack. Now he had zero idea where she'd gone. The boys took off with their marching orders, and he scanned the horizon. She was here somewhere. He kept himself low. He could hear the occasional paintball splat and ensuing groan by the player taken out of the game. He always took a moment to look up and make sure the boy was okay. He *was* chaperoning. He needed to remain cognizant of that. Playing the game was fun, but his chief goal was to keep these boys safe and unharmed in their play. Goal number two was taking out Ivy. Or not, he didn't actually *want* to shoot her with a paintball, he just—what? What did he want from Ivy? That was the real question he needed to answer, and not just in terms of paintball. Jaxon stayed to the outskirts, pensively watching the progress of the game.

When the sale of the building was complete, what then? He'd be on to his new life and Ivy would be left with what? Would she still have a business? He didn't trust wild-card Derrick Cross. He was beginning to think no one could, but was the man completely untrustworthy? Cross hadn't done anything shady. He was just brittle somehow, like he had a hidden agenda other than real estate acquisition.

Splat. Another one bites the dust.

Splat. Another one down.

Splat. And another one down.

As long as Ivy didn't bite the dust, he was okay with it.

Jaxon counted. Where were all the boys? He peered over at the seating area and counted the boys sprawled out chatting up Becca Whitaker. Twenty of them lounged in chairs, so that left four. Alden, Ronnie, Ivy and him.

The game was coming to a head. Jaxon eased toward the flag. Time to finish this. He popped up behind Ronnie. "Hey."

Ronnie about jumped out of his skin.

"It's just me. What's the plan?"

Ronnie's eyes lit up. "Really?"

"You're the captain."

Ronnie puffed up a little, and Jaxon smiled inwardly.

"It's just us on our team. The rest are out. They're hanging with Becca." Ronnie frowned, clearly envious of being left out of Rebecca holding court.

"You'll have your chance after," said Jaxon. "Now, let's get that flag."

They ran low along the fence line, ducking behind barrels and stacked pallets, peeking around corners. Ronnie was obviously having a fantastic time. It felt good to be one of the last men standing. They headed up the rise toward the flag. The coast was clear. No one had even spotted Alden and Ivy for at least forty-five minutes, but that didn't mean they were in the clear. Those two could be anywhere and...

Suddenly they materialized. Alden was covered in dirt and leaves, blending in with the terrain. And Ivy, Jaxon almost laughed when he saw her, was thoroughly covered in brambles. Despite her pincushion attire, she was majestic, brandishing her paint gun like a pro, sun glinting off her hair. The mask hid her face, so he couldn't see her expression.

Alden rose up and took aim at Ronnie just as Jaxon took aim at Alden. Ivy tilted her head at Jaxon and shook it. She pointed to herself and aimed her gun straight at Jaxon. He got her meaning even with the mask on.

*Let Alden win.*

He grinned. They needed to act quick. Splat went Alden's gun—Ronnie was out. In unison, they tilted their guns up, aimed at each other. In the last instant Jaxon dipped his gun and let his paintball fly at Ivy's foot.

Splat right on her shoe just as Splat!, a hit straight to his heart.

Alden grabbed the flag, whooping and running for his base, last man standing, and clearly the winner.

Ivy pulled off her mask.

"Thank you! What better time to win paintball than on his birthday? I was hoping, and then I saw you, and I just knew you understood my signals."

With a groan of disgust at Ivy's excited spiel, Ronnie stomped off with a backward comment. "You can have her."

"What does he mean by that?"

Jaxon shrugged. "Oh, you know, kids."

"I'm thrilled Alden won."

"Me too." They grinned, basking in the moment.

He glanced over and saw Ronnie boasting to Rebecca how he almost won the game.

Jaxon ruefully rubbed the paint spot on his shirt. "You hit me straight in the heart."

Ivy bit her lip. "Did I?"

Jaxon swallowed. He needed to get back to chaperoning. He muttered, "You have no idea."

# Chapter Seventeen

TIRED, BUT STILL jazzed after her paintball success, Ivy decided to pop into the tea shop on her way home. She adored the building with its quaint style, cheerful, striped awning, and how peaceful it was when she was there by herself. She could ponder her afternoon, and maybe make sense of the sizzling chemistry between her and Jaxon. Just after sunset, dusky blue encroached on the bright orange and mauve streaks high over the square. She stepped into her shop and froze.

She wasn't alone.

Her heart rate picked up. Her breath grew short as her fingers grappled for the light switch. She released her breath in a whoosh as she recognized Holly seated at the back table, still in her pink smock.

"Good lord, you scared me. What are you doing so late in my shop?" Ivy pressed a hand to her chest and took a couple of breaths to steady herself. She let the door swing closed and stepped inside to plop her purse and jacket on the counter by the register. It was unusual for Holly to work past three in the afternoon, since she rose well before dawn to begin the day's baking. Holly, alone, in the dark could not be good. It meant Holly was in a mood. And, Holly in a mood meant...

Her sister spoke, and her voice had that grating edge Ivy hated. *Here it comes*, she thought, and deflated in anticipation of total negativity. Really, it had been such a fabulous day, and now her sister would ruin it. Ivy tensed, prepared for the customary tirade. Of course, Holly would be angry about Ivy stealing her customers, even if it hadn't been on purpose. It was always a contest. If Ivy succeeded, Holly must not be. Ivy was tired of the tightrope walk between success and pleasing her sister. Success didn't need to be an either-or proposition. Shoulders hunched in preparation of Holly's verbal attack, she missed Holly's initial words and paused as what her sister had said sunk in.

"I'm sorry. Can you repeat that?"

"You need to be more careful."

Okay, not totally negative, but it might be interpreted as a threat. Not her sister's usual style, but...

"All these dates," Holly continued, waving a hand in the air. "I heard about the brawling in the square. It's all over town."

*Who would have shared that?* She certainly hadn't, and she couldn't imagine Jaxon telling anyone. Kyle and Pedro definitely wouldn't want it to get out. Fighting was bad for business.

"Dina," Ivy said aloud.

"Cece cut my hair while Dina was getting a perm."

Of course. That juicy bit of gossip would've been too good to not pass on. Dina was not known for restraint. If she hadn't already made the rounds to all the businesses on the square, sharing it at Cece's Salon would do the trick. Soon the whole town would know men were fighting over Ivy.

"You could've been hurt." It came out on a wail, as if the idea of Ivy being hurt was painful to Holly.

"I wasn't the one brawling." Ivy hung up her jacket, put her bag under the counter, and put water on for tea. She chose a pink, floral teapot, perfect for two, and filled it with hot water to sit until the kettle boiled. She set about creating her special tea blend planned for the fundraiser. By reflex, she glanced at the shelf where her magic cookies waited in the clear glass cookie jar with its pretty etched design until the moment she would gift them. She hadn't decided how to package them for Jaxon, or even if she should.

"Wait!" The etched cookie jar was gone. She knew she'd placed it smack dab in the middle of the shelf. She'd tied a pretty green and pink ribbon on the rim.

Ivy glanced around. She reached up and hurriedly began to shift items on the shelf. She was certain she hadn't moved it, and it was too big to be hidden from sight. She stepped closer to extend her reach and felt a tiny crunch under her foot. She stepped back and felt another. She focused her gaze at the floor and spotted a glass shard. Then another in the kick space under the counter.

Had it broken? "My etched jar!" It had been a gift on her last birthday. Aunt Lydia had had the cookie press design etched into the jar.

"Sorry. It fell."

Ivy blinked at her sister.

"Well, flew off, more like. It was the weirdest thing. I was in the back, just there in our shared space, minding my own business, totaling up my own receipts when I glanced up. That shelf—" she waved a hand at it in her way "—was right in my line of sight and the moment my eyes landed on the cookie jar it leaped off, sailed right through the air. No one was anywhere near it. It just committed hari kari and flung itself off the shelf. I swear. I cleaned up the mess. Most of the cookies fell on the counter, above where the jar crashed into smithereens on the floor. But the cookies were all broken and crumbly. It isn't like you could serve them to customers."

Ivy's gut churned. She wasn't sure if she was more upset about the jar breaking or the cookie disaster. She should be more upset about the jar, but somehow the loss of the cookies made her sad, like her hopes had been dashed. "Did you throw them away?" All that work gone to waste—an omen she should have left well enough alone. Just like every single member of the Hazard Historical Society had cautioned her. It wasn't meant to be.

She and Jaxon were not meant to be.

Except today, they'd had such fun making sure Alden

came out on top. Sacrificing themselves so Alden had the best birthday ever. It was so them. She smiled, remembering their shared moment. As soon as their eyes met, they'd known what the other was thinking. It had been perfect.

Something Holly said made her pause. *It isn't like you could serve them to customers.*

Well, no, of course not. She had never meant them to be for customers, but had Holly really thrown them away? Ivy focused in on her sister at the table. Directly in front of Holly was a gallon jug of milk, a glass half full and a pretty little rose-patterned china plate covered in crumbs.

*Oh no.*

Holly's mouth curved in a sheepish smile. She shrugged one shoulder. "I ate 'em. Such a shame to let them go to waste. They smelled amazing. I swear, it's like the jar jumped off the counter to get to me. Only me. Like these amazing cookies were meant for me all this time. I bet if we sold these, business would go through the roof. But you won't share, will you? Well, it doesn't matter. I know your secret. Your cookies had all my favorite flavors. Cinnamon, nutmeg—really a lot of nutmeg, which is surprising. Don't pout at me like that. I already know you won't share the magic recipe with me."

*Magic?* The kettle began to shrill. Ivy jumped, grabbed a hot pad, and jerked it off the burner. *What did Holly know?*

"I'm sure they are *very special*. Probably one of the recipes Mom gave you instead of me." The edge in her voice was back.

"You got everything else." The words were out before Ivy could pull them back. But instead of it leading to an argument with Holly denying she was the favored daughter, her sister just rolled her eyes. "Anyway, I was careful not to eat glass. I'm not stupid. I tossed the ones that fell on the floor. I swept up all the mess from your flying cookie jar. Well, most of it. Once I tasted a cookie, I was through cleaning." Holly smacked her lips. "But I did analyze the flavors." She grinned. "I think I've got it figured. I might even give you a run for your money." She smirked, "Cardamom, right?"

"Right." Ivy agreed absently. "Um, you really ate them?"

"Don't get all huffy. They weren't any good for anyone else."

Ivy set about brewing a pot of tea, dumping off the hot water to warm the pot. Giving up on her special tea blend for now, she mixed white tea with hibiscus because she needed to de-stress. She added the loose tea leaves to the pot, pouring boiling water over them. Something about her sister's statement rang true.

What did it mean, that the cookies were no good for anyone else? She had been thinking about Holly and singing the blessing while she baked them. Did that make them for her sister? What had Ivy been thinking about the first time she baked the cookies? Jaxon, for sure, but also about improving her business.

Just how magic was the magic of Hazard?

It might bear more research to find out. Maybe she

needed to control her thoughts when she was baking. Making another batch of cookies could be a science experiment. Kind of like how she blended her teas. She had loved science in school. It had been her favorite. Chemistry class especially, with its trial and error and testing, not to mention the occasional explosion. Really, blending tea took a lot of mixing and taste-testing, and baking could be an experiment. Well, the way she baked. Not the way Holly baked. Holly followed recipes and rules.

Ivy set the teapot on the tablecloth in front of her sister. She gathered rose-patterned cups and saucers to match and sat across from Holly.

Holly reached over the table and clasped her hands before she could pour. "You need to be more careful. Really, please let me know when you're going on a date. I need to know you get home safely. I waited up the other night until I heard you."

"I saw your light."

Holly nodded. "Dating is risky. The world's a precarious place. I'll watch out for you." Holly squeezed her hands before she let go.

"We're in Hazard. Nothing ever happens in Hazard." Ivy poured the tea and took a sip of her own. Yes, now calmer, she breathed out and in, that's what she needed. A spot of tea to calm down.

Holly shoved her cup away. "Obviously, it does. Now there's brawling in the street. Dina said she'd never seen

Pedro so jacked up, and you know how he gets. I mean, he's pretty hyped all the time, so for Dina to think it was over the top, it really must've been crazy."

Ivy's head was swimming, so she tuned out her sister. Holly had never been concerned about her before, not like this. Not enough to keep tabs on her for safety's sake. No, that was a bit of a role reversal.

"I know you want to win the silly bet you talked me into, but is it worth dating crazy people? What were you thinking? Pedro and Kyle?"

"We went to school with Pedro and Kyle. I've known them for years." They'd never been interested in Ivy before. They'd been jocks, and she'd been warming the bleachers. Hmm, she was still like that, but Jaxon actually noticed her in the bleachers. Holly was still rambling.

"It's just the two of us, with Mom and Dad cruising 'round the world."

"What about Aunt Lydia?"

Holly waved a dismissive hand. "She's not focused on us. She's all about fun and smelling the flowers, not to mention her historical society. Really, it's just us. I don't know what I would do without you."

A happy dance, thought Ivy, before acknowledging that was unfair. She imagined her own life without Holly's constant criticism. For one crystal clear instant, she enjoyed that thought, then put it aside. She adored her sister. Holly had been a stabilizing influence all her life. She loved having her around and sharing space for their similar businesses. And Holly really did love her, even if they bickered all the time. "I don't know what I would do without you either."

Holly nodded and picked up some crumbs off the plate and ate them. She rolled her eyes in ecstasy and sighed. "So, you'll be careful, right? I'm sorry I was critical of you. From now on, I'll protect you." She tilted her head. "I'll be your shield, little sister." She nodded, clearly pleased by her proclamation. "Don't go out with any more losers."

"I wouldn't call them losers."

"You're too charitable. This is Hazard, and dating is hazardous. You need to stay safe. We could hang out."

"Hang out," Ivy repeated stupidly. *Holly wanted to hang out with her?*

"I could help you with your marketing."

Ivy leaned back to study her sister. "That would be great, but what about the bet?"

"Well, I don't *really* want you to fail, do I? That would be petty."

Petty was Holly's middle name, or it had been. Had eating the cookies changed their relationship? "You would really lose the bet."

Displeasure, quickly cloaked, flashed over Holly's face. "We'll just cancel that silly old bet," said Holly.

"Ah." There it was. Holly couldn't lose, if the bet was no more.

"I'll help you succeed instead. That'll be better. It'll just be us." Again with the hand clasping. "We've always been devoted to each other, even as kids. We can be devoted to each other now. Have each other's backs. What do you say?"

# Chapter Eighteen

JAXON FINISHED THE architectural plans for the kitchen addition he'd been working on for Cece Tollivar. She wanted to surprise her contractor husband Dartagnan in the hope he would actually upgrade her kitchen, like he'd been promising for the last five years. Jaxon was glad for the work, but wasn't sure Cece was pursuing her goal the proper way. He knew *he* didn't like to be tricked, coerced, or blindsided.

He paused at the salon's entrance, and she waved him in. "Hey, Jaxxy—you got my plans all drawn up?"

"Sure do. You positive Dart'll go for you surprising him like this?"

"Ah, that don't matter." Cece laughed. "A promise is a promise. I'm just helping my man keep his." She took the envelope with the plans from Jaxon and spread them out on the counter. "You sure do detailed work. I love the arch here over the little breakfast nook for two. So romantic. Makes me excited about getting up early, just so we can enjoy breakfast together. Do I owe you anything?"

"Nope, you're all paid up."

"Even better. Thank you for being a co-conspirator in

my underhandedness."

Jaxon shifted. Underhandedness? He was just doing a job. He sure hoped Dart understood. He especially hoped it was a pleasant surprise and not an annoyance. But doing the right thing could lead to pitfalls. Jaxon preferred to be upfront, which meant he'd better quit procrastinating and tell *all* his tenants about the sale of the building. Might as well start now. "I need to fill you in on some changes."

"With the plans?" Cece squinted at the blueprints.

"No, with this building. I'm selling."

"Selling?" Cece straightened her chartreuse-framed glasses to peer at him.

Jaxon nodded. "I've taken a job in Boston. It'll be too hard to manage the building long distance. I don't want to shortchange my tenants. I've got a buyer and escrow started."

"Oh, well, life is change." Cece studied him. "You don't look so happy. Are you?"

"Yes?" Jaxon coughed. He hadn't meant for it to sound like a question. The closer it got to his move, the more he doubted his decision. He had a new salaried job and a lead on an apartment that allowed pets. It'd be close enough to walk to work if the weather was good. He loved being able to walk to work like he did here. Of course, it wouldn't be as close. Montgomery would be alone longer than he was used to, but there was a park. Just not right across the street like the town green.

He'd checked out the nearby shops and restaurants. It'd

be great. He could experience all Boston had to offer: museums and public transport…and traffic and crowds. He frowned. "Anyway, I wanted to let my tenants know about the sale. I told Holly when I was in the bakery. I'm headed to tell Lydia next, probably."

"And Ivy?" Cece's glasses slid down her nose.

Jaxon shifted under the older woman's perusal. "Of course, I'll tell Ivy."

"If you told Holly, won't Ivy already know?"

One would think, but Jaxon was pretty sure Holly was keeping it from Ivy for her own reasons in her one-upmanship way.

"Lydia probably already knows, too," Cece pointed out.

"I'll keep you informed, and let you know when the sale's final."

"Guess I can expect a rent increase." Cece sighed. "Oh well, nothing stays the same."

Jaxon headed to Lydia's. He paused outside Ivy's shop, but it looked as if she was cleaning in the back, so he moved on to LaFleur.

The door chimed like a doorbell as he entered and stopped to take it all in. It amused him how differently each tenant arranged the nearly identical spaces. Cece's salon appeared long and thin, with haircutting stations down one side and shampoo bowls down the other. Holly's bakery looked square, with a counter cutting the space in half and all the space before it open and empty to accommodate early morning crowds.

Lydia's space could best be described as jungle-themed secret garden. Towering tropical plants interspersed with local flora reigned, the clutter rather like its proprietress. Glass shelves packed and nearly overflowing miraculously highlighted each trinket for sale. A glassed room in the middle, filled with blooms of every variety, made the shop smell floral and earthy—a bit like Lydia, who frequently over-applied her perfume but maintained a practical down-to-earth mien.

Had Holly told her great-aunt about Jaxon selling the building? Lydia, not one to leave a thought unsaid, hadn't approached him. He wound through the densely packed shop to find Lydia at a back counter, flower cuttings spread before her. Two completed arrangements of a dozen roses loomed, one in deep red, another in white.

"Those are lovely," he said.

"They're for the two leads in the play Ivy saw. She asked me to send them flowers to congratulate them for a successful run. The red ones are for Tessa, who played Irene Adler, and the white are for Chad, who played Sherlock Holmes. What can I arrange for you?"

"I'm not here for flowers today." Was he ever? Jaxon couldn't remember ever ordering from her shop. Candace never had any use for flowers, considered anything that could die a waste of time. She preferred money spent on experiences. But couldn't receiving flowers be an experience? "I wanted to let you know I'm leaving Hazard and selling the building."

"No," said Lydia. "Oh, no, no, that's wrong."

"No, I am."

She shook her head with emphasis.

"Lydia, I know what my plans are. Escrow will be closing…" But Lydia was shaking her head. She waved a hand at him to stop.

"You don't know." Lydia pressed her lips tight. "Fine. Make your plans. Fine." She went back to stabbing a third set of roses into the vase she had set up. Despite her obvious agitation, each rose went in straight, perfect, and flawless. Even upset, Lydia knew her business. "Who wants to buy your building? Not that horrible Derrick Cross."

"Well, yes."

Lydia's lips got tighter.

"How do you know Derrick?"

"Man made an offer on Oleander House before I joined the historical society. I didn't trust him to do right by my house. Even if I'd sold it, I'd want it preserved. That Mr. Cross, well…" Her lips pinched tighter until they were a thin red slash. "Next, he tried to purchase Sundial Sands. As if! Hazel will never sell that Gilded Age beauty. She grew up there as a girl. It's her grandson's last connection to his parents, after they perished in that frightful accident. That stuffy Mr. Cross even made an offer on the Hazard Inn, but the buyer chose someone out of New York. Kate somebody, who actually wants to be an innkeeper. I don't trust that Cross man's motives."

"Most of the women in town find him charming."

"Don't patronize an old woman. Do *you* find him charming?"

Jaxon wasn't sure how to respond to that. "It's a business deal."

"Yes, yes, well, you'll see, won't you?" She stopped stabbing roses and started fluffing up ferns. "Have you told my nieces?"

"Holly, I told Holly."

"And Ivy?"

Lydia's intent gaze made Jaxon shift. What was it with these older women and their piercing gazes? He'd swear they saw straight into his soul to his attraction for Ivy Wayland.

"I plan to go there next. I just told Cece."

"And passed Ivy on your way to tell me? Why ever would you do that?"

"She looked busy."

Lydia raised a brow. Her gaze swept over the cuttings scattered in front of her.

Point taken. "I'll just let myself out."

BRANTLEY MITCHELL HOVERED outside Ivy's shop door for the umpteenth time that afternoon. Ivy found his ballet of indecision baffling. Brantley would start to enter her shop, then step away, then again turn as if to enter before spinning away in the opposite direction. This go-round, he loped across the street and sat on the bench by the statue of Eddie, hands clasped on knees. Suddenly electrified, he jumped up, crossed back to the tea shop with purpose, only to again hover outside her door, vibrating like a dragonfly. It was hypnotic. She wasn't a scary person. She had cultivated a warm, convivial demeanor. She loved welcoming customers. Why didn't he just come in?

When Ivy could no longer stand it, she grabbed the glass cleaner and a rag. She waited until he was nearly to the door and jerked it open. "Oh, Brantley." She feigned surprise and graced him with a bright smile. "Come in." She preceded him and hoped he would follow. When he trotted after her, she motioned him to a table. "What brings you in today?"

"Priscilla said I should."

That stopped Ivy for a moment. Hard to fathom Pricilla Whitaker sending business her way. Ivy gave herself a mental head shake. "Oh, well, can I get you something?"

"Yes, please." He nodded and sat, hands clasped on the table like a good boy. Ivy almost laughed. He was her last customer of the day. But a customer, even a socially awkward one, was still a customer.

When she waited, he said, "Can I have a cup of tea and one of those?" He pointed to the scones under the glass dome.

"Of course." Ivy fixed him a soothing blend of chamomile and peppermint tea along with a warmed raspberry scone on a sturdy stoneware plate, and brought it out as his left foot bounced under the table.

Brantley was always so solemn. People considered him offish, but Ivy suspected he was just shy. A local silversmith, specializing in eighteenth century reproductions, he had a studio workshop two blocks off the square. She'd seen him play on the Rebels baseball team—well, mostly sit on the bench. They never put him up to bat that she could recall, although she remembered him playing shortstop. Brantley was strong, his art required it of him, but a bit gangly.

He took a sip of tea and a bite of scone. He chewed and swallowed, hard. "Will you go out with me?"

The question caught Ivy off guard. "Oh, I…"

"Are you into history? We could tour a mansion? Here, I mean, not in Newport. I wouldn't expect you to go to Newport with me."

"My family owns one of the mansions."

"Sorry, never mind, you've probably seen them already."

"No, actually. I haven't toured any. They've been under renovation as long as I can remember and only recently opened for tours. My aunt's part of the Hazard Historical Society, and she's been after me to see the mansion she manages. Are you familiar with Oleander House?"

"I restored a set of goblets for the historical society and made some re-creation candlesticks for the mantel."

"Did you? That's fabulous. Oleander House is completely refurbished. How wonderful that you were part of that. I've only seen a couple rooms, but they have a new docent. Sorry, I'm babbling."

"No," he said, and wiped his mouth with a napkin. "I'd love to take you to tour your family's ancestral home. Oh, that sounded odd. I'm sorry."

"Don't be. It sounds lovely. Thank you."

"How about Thursday? Do they do tours late enough?"

"I'll check. I'm sure it can be arranged. Thank you for thinking of me."

Aunt Lydia would be ecstatic, although Ivy wasn't sure if Malory would. As much as Ivy admired her, Malory remained a formidable enigma, even after their milkshake excursion. But she probably knew Brantley if he'd done silverwork for Oleander House.

What Ivy refused to do was ask Holly's permission to go on a date. What possible danger could an afternoon house tour represent? She had successfully fended off unwanted advances by the Rebels first, second, and third basemen. Surely she had nothing to worry about with Brantley Mitchell, Rebels's shortstop.

After Brantley finished up his snack and she closed the door behind him, she called her aunt about touring the mansion Thursday.

"Let me schedule a private tour for you."

"I don't like to be a bother. I'd rather join an existing

tour if there's an opening."

"I'll check online. Yes, we have a tour with two spots left Thursday at four. If it's not late enough…"

"I'll make it work." She didn't want to put out her new friend, and alone on a tour with Brantley—well—this was better, to be part of a crowd. Being on a date with an uptight, fidgety person would be better in a group rather than alone, surely.

Ivy was pondering this when Jaxon stopped outside her door. One look at him, and the tension just drained out of her. He had that effect. She hadn't realized how anxious her brief time with Brantley had made her.

Jaxon motioned at his dog. "Want to take a turn around the square?"

"Love to." Ivy grabbed a sweater and locked up. The breezy afternoon was a perfect excuse to step out with the only man she wanted to spend time with. They stepped straight out to the green and began to stroll around the outside. The breeze buffeting in gusts, Ivy smoothed her hair, but tendrils escaped from her ponytail until she gave up and set it free.

The expression on Jaxon's face was priceless.

"You didn't know, did you?"

He opened his mouth and closed it. "What do you mean?" His eyes on her hair, as it churned like Medusa's in a tempest, made Ivy laugh. "That I'm a wild woman?"

His eyes grew warmer as he gazed at her. "Wild, is that so?"

"I keep it tamed, but on a day like this?" She shrugged. "Why try?"

"You should let your hair down more often."

"Figuratively or literally?"

"Both."

They walked companionably along Worthy Street, Montgomery trotting ahead and occasionally pausing to sniff. They turned at Endeavor, passing the thrift store. At Throckmorton Grocery, Montgomery strained at his leash, but Jaxon held him in check.

"The grocery must smell good to him."

"It's the meat counter, and the fresh fish." At Toby and Mac's, the dog settled.

"I heard our barkeeps may tie the knot."

"Seriously? Mackenna doesn't seem the marrying type, but I'm not much for town gossip."

"I hear it in the tea shop."

"I try to avoid it."

Ivy tilted her head in an unspoken question.

"I don't like how I figure into it, like I'm pathetic."

"No one thinks that."

He raised a skeptical brow. "I'll need to move for a fresh start. Can't remake yourself in a small town."

"I've lived here since fifth grade and remade myself many times."

At Jaxon's raised brow, she added, "You want a run-down?"

"I do, I really do."

"In middle school I was very into mermaids, so my mom helped me color my hair blue green. By the time I got to ninth grade, I had changed that up for a fascination with mythology and wood nymphs."

"Nymphs?"

At his joking leer, she laughed. "Not that kind of nymph. I was only fourteen. Don't tease; this was serious stuff. I fancied myself a dryad, you know, like the spirits of trees. On May Day, I passed out flowers."

"How did that go over with your classmates?"

"You can imagine, can't you? Although I will say, they all wanted a flower. They thought I was crazy, but they didn't want to be excluded from my flower-bestowing. Holly ran with the popular crowd, so I was a continual embarrassment."

"You were imaginative."

"By the time I graduated, I had changed it up again, and I was all about the environment and saving the forests. After graduation, I bumped around for a few years volunteering in the community and trying different jobs. I worked briefly in a Goth clothing store. I was a receptionist at a veterinary clinic. I waited tables at Leo's diner. Finally, I went away and took business classes before I came back home to open the tea shop. In fact, this spring, I believe it's time for a new me. Perhaps it's time for a new you, too." *Or a new us.*

Jaxon fell silent and focused on Montgomery trotting

along, blissfully unaware of the sudden undercurrent between them. Had she shared too much? Jaxon was so easy to talk to. He always acted so interested in what she had to say.

Jaxon glanced over at her and, for an instant, she got lost in his eyes.

He coughed and took a breath. "I love springtime," he said. "The wind—what is it with wind and springtime?"

"Winds of change bring the hope and promise of what will be."

"I wanted to talk to you about that. About…change."

"I like change," Ivy said decisively.

"You do?" He angled his head, and Ivy had to think about her statement. "Change within parameters. I love it here in Hazard. I don't plan to change that. I do enjoy changing up my menu and planning for the future."

"About that."

"Thank you for the new lease. I feel secure knowing it's squared away. Such a good omen. Business has picked up. I can't believe how transformative new menu items are. I should've done it long ago. I even had a new customer from out of town, who's purchasing property in the area."

She cast a side glance at Jaxon who started coughing again. Ivy patted him on the back. "Are you alright?"

Jaxon made a strangled sound, even as he kept walking. Montgomery stopped to sniff the grass. "Did he say what his name was?"

"Derrick, I think. He only wanted a scone, said he wasn't

much of a tea drinker. I tried to convince him to try a cup of a new blend I've been working on. I just added some Earl Grey to it. I expect I'll have it perfected soon. I used to love chemistry class and this feels a little bit like that."

At Jaxon's expression of genuine interest, Ivy tingled to her toes. "You want to know about my tea blend?"

"Sure."

"Lots of science involved. I'm working to create an aromatic calming combination. I've decided to establish a house blend and thought I would name the best ones I've created so far. But naming is harder than I thought it would be."

"Like what have you come up with?"

"Peacemaker?"

Jaxon shook his head.

"How about Serenity?"

"That was a sci-fi movie."

"You would know that. Okay, how about Quietude? Calm with attitude?"

Jaxon shook his head in mock horror.

Ivy laughed. "Okay, so, not good."

"What if you incorporated the history of the area? Georgian Colonial blend or Rebel blend," he suggested.

"I'd need to do more research." Ivy was delighted with the idea of a Georgian Colonial blend. It was right in step with what she'd suggested at the board meeting. Her mind took off imagining her successful new tea blend at the fundraiser, combined with her scones and savory sandwiches.

But which scone and which sandwich and…

Jaxon was watching her.

"Sorry, my mind's running a mile a minute. I offered to help with refreshments for the fundraiser. I can't wait to introduce my new Georgian Colonial blend." She gave a happy little jump.

"Excellent idea." As Jaxon gazed at Ivy, he knew he needed to share that he was leaving, but she was so caught up in the moment. He hated to rain on her enthusiasm.

"You inspired it," she said.

"Me?" Jaxon opened his mouth to admit he was leaving, but choked on the words. He couldn't bear to dim the light in her eyes.

"You're good for me."

Jaxon ignored the voice of self-recrimination and focused on Ivy's zeal instead. "Tell me more about the fundraiser."

# Chapter Nineteen

BRANTLEY INSISTED ON picking Ivy up for their date at her apartment, but she convinced him to meet at the tea shop. He drove up in a restored Model T Ford.

"Oh, my, this is lovely."

"I like restoration."

"An old-fashioned kind of guy."

Brantley ducked his head. He was silent on the drive out, which didn't surprise Ivy. He came across as reserved, but the silence didn't feel companionable like it did with Jaxon. This was strained to the point where Brantley's angst began to affect her. Ivy breathed a relieved sigh when they reached Oleander House.

The others had arrived, with Malory waiting only on Ivy and Brantley. Ivy started to apologize, but at Brantley's stiff posture fell silent, intuitively aware that apologizing would embarrass him. A private tour might've been better, but Ivy was just as glad to be part of the group.

She scoped out their tour companions. First was a couple in their sixties, formally attired for their anniversary celebration after, followed by a bevy of women in jeans, tank tops, and flirty dresses, all clearly together on a girls' trip. Overall, a total of eight made a fairly comfortable turnout to tour a mansion that hadn't even had its grand opening yet.

Malory was gracious, if overly solemn. Ivy could see why Hazel didn't favor her delivery, especially for Sundial Sands, but for Oleander House it worked, due to the mansion's murky past. In dour tones, Malory relayed the mansion's history, how Laurent LaFleur, fourth son of Henri and Giselle LaFleur, arrived in 1785 to make his fortune in the new world. His interest in shipping led him to commission ships to carry ginseng from the new world to China and bring tea, tableware, and spices to America. Laurent planned to bring his betrothed over, but she perished with her family and his in the French Revolution when his family's ancestral home was set aflame by an angry mob.

As the only remaining son to carry on the family name, he married a local girl, but the union ended tragically when she died of tea made from oleander leaves after the birth of their only child. The son took over the flourishing shipping company and christened the mansion Oleander House in homage to his mother.

Hmm, wondered Ivy, was owning a tea shop in poor taste considering her family history? Or did it bring the family history full circle?

Ivy adored traipsing through the rooms. Malory had done a stunning job showcasing tableware and sharing the history of the family's business. She related the stories of the marriages down through history. Ivy's Irish father wasn't mentioned but her mother was, having lived in the house as a toddler raised by Aunt Lydia until the house was shut down forty years ago when the upkeep grew too expensive.

Malory drew attention to Brantley's work and introduced him to the other tour members.

He blushed a deep red at being singled out. Malory singled out Ivy as well, making the others laugh and look askance when she mentioned her tea shop. Clearly, naming a blend for Oleander House was out of the question. What the tour lacked was a gift shop. Ivy planned to suggest it to the historical society.

She wasn't sure what Brantley had in mind next. He was so quiet. But he took her on a leisurely drive along the cliff, and it was breathtaking and beautiful, but also hushed and awkward. They wound up at Toby and Mac's, which seemed an odd choice, as the pub was known for being loud and lively. Brantley didn't seem the type, but he had her car door open and ushered her inside so quickly it left no chance to suggest another venue.

Music was several decibels above conversation level, blasting out "Rock and a Hard Place." Ivy spotted three of the Roadies in skinny jeans and halter tops huddled at the bar. Brantley pulled Ivy behind him to tuck in at a teetering table in an alcove. When Mac swung by, Brantley ordered mussels and mojitos for two. Ivy almost spoke up but shrugged it off. She was oddly relieved to see Jaxon at the table with Roman, now free of his crutches. She could just make out a bit of their conversation, of Roman talking a mile a minute about door latches.

After ordering, Brantley excused himself, and the Roadies descended on Ivy's table.

"So, Ive, we see you're hangin' with the Rebels's shortstop," said Nell, star hitter for the Roadies and leader of Hazard's road crew.

"Have a seat," Ivy said to the three women, who had already collected chairs and made themselves comfy at her table the minute Brantley was out of sight.

"How's it going?" asked Tessa, eyeing Ivy intently.

Mimicking them, Ivy leaned in. "Why the interest?"

"Oh, well, we were all in Cece's when Dina came in, and you know Dina," said Tylene.

"We just wanted to warn you," said Nell.

"About?"

"Brantley," they chimed in unison.

"Solidarity, you understand," Tylene said.

"We like you, and we get that you're makin' the rounds and all."

Ivy's gaze swiveled back to Nell. "The rounds?"

"With the Rebel hotties."

"Oh, well…"

"No worries, it's cool," continued Nell.

"We did too when we first moved here. They're good-lookin' guys, but…" Tylene snorted, "they tend to represent the positions they play a teeny bit too well."

Nods followed all around.

Nell must've read Ivy's look of confusion. "Kyle's the pitcher and, boy, did he throw out at Pedro. Pedro's a hard hitter."

Ivy blanched. "Surely they didn't hit you when you went out?"

"No, we're talking 'bout the brawl."

Ivy nodded. "Ah, Dina."

"She's the blabbiest," said Tessa. "But you know how, like, Roman goes for first base and Joel's a second base kind of guy."

"And Rob goes straight for third base?" finished Ivy.

"See, I knew she'd get it," said Tylene to the others.

Brantley still wasn't back, and Ivy was having fun now. "Okay, so Brantley plays short stop, right? So does he stop short?"

Nell let out a hoot. "No, Ive, no, no, no. Brant's the master of the double play. You'll need to watch yourself from all sides. Well, unless you're into that, which is cool, too. That's all we wanted to say."

"Bye!" They jumped up and scurried back to the bar, just as Brantley got back to the table in time for Mackenna to swing by with his order.

Brantley slurped mussels while Ivy sipped her mojito. When she stood and excused herself to use the restroom, Brantley rose. Ivy thought he was being polite, but the creepy factor rose exponentially as he trailed her down the long hallway. When she glanced back in question, he stepped close and said, "I had a nice time."

"I did too, Brantley."

Suddenly, he transformed into octopus man, his strong hands coming at her, aiming for second and third base. Ivy stumbled backward and found herself trapped between her date and a brick wall. She cast her gaze in search of a way to sidestep, but Brantley loomed. She immediately understood why the Roadies had warned her. Ivy put her hand out to nudge him back.

"Hey, Brant."

Someone slapped Brantley on the back. Ivy peered past his shoulder and was never more grateful to see Jaxon in her life. Roman was there, too, and easing Brantley to the side to pull him into a conversation. Their agile moves gave Ivy enough space to slip out and hightail it for the women's while Roman talked a steady stream and Jaxon steered Brantley toward the front.

Alone, Ivy stared at herself in the mirror in the glaring light. How she hated the dating game's expectations and posturing. All at once, everything Holly said about the dangers of dating flooded her thoughts. Ivy leaned on the sink and took a breath. Steadier, she stepped in the hallway and out the back into the night.

As the door slammed shut, a deep voice rumbled. "You okay?"

Ivy jumped and let out a squeal.

"Whoa, sorry. I didn't mean to scare you."

Hand on her chest trying to calm her raging heartbeat, Ivy recognized Jaxon. He was leaning against the building, the concern in his eyes clear. Her heart rate eased at the realization he had been waiting to make certain she was all right. She let out a breath and nodded. "You knew I'd abscond."

"He deserves it," said Jaxon in a growl of disapproval, as he pushed off from the wall.

"He still in there?"

"Roman will keep him occupied all evening. He's good at that."

Ivy and Jaxon fell into step and rounded the building to the square. "If we're walking, do you want to get Montgomery?" she asked.

"Nah, he's on a playdate." Ivy knew she must've appeared confused when he added, "With Cece's dogs."

"Ah." Ivy blew out a sigh when she spotted the town green and the statue. With Jaxon at her side, she didn't want to be anywhere else.

"Are you sure you're okay? He's lousy with social signals."

"Thanks for the rescue. Do you do this for all of Brantley's dates?"

"Can I ask why you went out with him?"

"I'm pretty sure Priscilla set me up."

"Pris, as in Alden's mom?"

"Long story," said Ivy at Jaxon's raised eyebrow.

"I've got time."

"It's a high school story," said Ivy.

"Okay, I've got lots of time." Jaxon grinned.

Ivy studied him to see if he was serious before she shrugged and launched into the small-town dynamics of going through school with people you'd known your whole life.

Jaxon shook his head in wonder. "I must've moved a dozen times as a kid. I never experienced half that."

"Lucky you," Ivy joked.

He tilted his head. "Not really."

"Was it hard to be the new kid?"

"Harder to *always* be the new kid. That's why I hoped I could belong here."

"You do belong here."

Jaxon shook his head. "Not like you." He gazed at her in a way Ivy couldn't fathom, with longing and sadness.

"Here's your tea shop and your car. I should let you go." He gave a nod and raised a hand in farewell. "Until the fundraiser."

He strode off before Ivy could invite him in. She shrugged, tucked herself inside her tea shop, and decided to relegate her miserable date to a lesson learned and use the time to create an ideal tea blend. She needed it ready for the fundraiser. Instead, she found herself mixing up dough for her Very Special Cookies. She knew it was a bad idea, an addiction she should forgo. Every time she baked the cookies it went awry, her serene life growing more complex with each batch. She couldn't stop herself. She knew the recipe by heart.

Drafts kicked up as she stirred, alternately pulling and pushing at the glass door until the building breathed.

Ivy started out humming and then sang. Rain tapping in sprinkles expanded to splashy droplets blown sideways, splatting on the picture window.

Swaying in time to the gusts rattling the door, she started to dance. Electric air sizzled.

Ivy let her hair swing loose. In riotous waves around her head, it began to float.

Lightning cracked, illuminating the tea shop in stark clarity.

Thunder answered. Its deep rumbles reminded her of Jaxon's voice reverberating within her when he spoke, how he'd rescued her and made her safe. How his presence protected her from Brantley's unwelcome advances.

Had she given out the wrong signals? On every date? She should speak up, be more assertive. She'd meant to, but she had spent the last three years perfecting her welcoming demeanor as she built up an essentially superfluous business in a small town. Had dating again all been a colossal waste of time? None of these guys were Jaxon. Somehow, even when she didn't speak up, Jaxon was in tune. He knew.

Would she give *these* cookies to Jaxon? Should she even try?

She had no clue what the results of this night would be. Maybe she'd eat all the cookies. She could be devoted to herself, selfish, doing as she pleased, caring not a whit what anyone else thought. That sounded magnificent. But she knew it would never happen. It simply was not who she was.

Tonight felt portentous, larger, more. Somehow her business depended on this night going forward. And that made no sense whatsoever. So, in the midst of the biggest storm yet this month, Ivy came into her own. With a generous smattering of nutmeg, she mixed and she chilled the dough. She sang and she shaped the cookies. She used the time in between to create the most perfect of all tea blends and she knew it was right. It was *the* one, her own unique tea blend, featuring all her favorites: Darjeeling and mint, oolong and clove, a touch of tangerine, with three secret dashes of this, that, and the other. A secret blend.

To the crack of lightning and rumble of thunder, the blessing flowed forth from her lips in melody, her feet tapping out the rhythm in dance. As she pressed the pattern—the most perfect pattern—and sprinkled cardamom, she relived her life, remembering childhood joy, teenage angst, and the freedom of adulthood. To percussive wind, harmony of storm, and melody of the Hazard Blessing, she baked cookies, celebrating all that life had to offer, and each tray revealed cookies of absolute, flawless perfection.

She let them cool and set about making herself a pot with her new blend. She chose her ivy-patterned teapot. Wind swirled and eased, the rattling door a past phenomenon. Calm now, she packed the cookies in a plain white bakery box and tied it with a green velvet ribbon, then decided on the ideal name for her new blend. She didn't know what she was doing, but she was doing it anyway. Perhaps it should be her new motto. Somehow, somewhere, some way, everyone needed to do the same.

Find Your Way.

Ivy set the box of her latest batch of magical cookies under the counter and stepped out onto the dampened sidewalk, the clouds dark and drifting silently above. She drove home through the sleeping town to her lonely apartment. When she arrived to trudge up the metal grillwork steps and let herself into her place, Holly's light was off, her sister's apartment quiet and still. But that was to be expected. Ivy hadn't asked her sister to wait up, to make certain she made it home safe.

# Chapter Twenty

THE DAY OF the first Annual Hazard Historical Society Fundraiser dawned in a stunning array of color. The red-streaked sunrise didn't bode well for clear weather, but once the sun was fully above the horizon, the sky transformed into a brilliant blue with big, fluffy, white clouds wafting overhead. Ivy chose a flowy, spring calico dress in sage and pink with apple-green accents. Dressing in her tearoom colors was part of her marketing plan. She would take a cue from Holly and be her own live advertisement.

She'd been up late baking for the event but was wide awake and ready. She had blueberry scones, ginger crinkles, and savory meat pies, all individually packaged in little white sleeves stamped with the Ivy Way Tea Shop.

Before she locked her front door, wind buffeted against her as if to say hello, so she grabbed a fluffy emerald sweater and shrugged it on to keep back the chill. The day's weather might be a bit too blustery. Fingers crossed, Ivy hoped it wouldn't be breezy out at Oleander House, but Malory had promised to open up the courtyard, and that should shield the guests from the worst of the wind.

Holly, of course, had already headed out much earlier to pack up her goods for the event and instruct her employees on what she expected them to accomplish while she was away for the day. Hollister's Bakery would be open, but Ivy would leave her shop closed. There was only so much of her to go around. They'd agreed to ride together in the bakery van to the event and despite Holly's sudden change of attitude, she wouldn't put it past Holly to leave her stranded, trying to transport all her baked goods in her tiny little car if she showed up late.

Ivy arrived at the shops to find everything, even her own items, packed up in the van, and Holly, foot tapping and waiting.

"You don't need to go in your shop. I took care of everything—well, I had my employees take care of everything. Get in. We need to go."

"Wait, I just want to check…"

"Don't you trust me?" Holly's intensity indicated that the wrong answer would lead to an unpleasant ride over.

"Of…course, I just think I should…"

"We don't have time for that."

Her sister hadn't even listened to what she was about to say. Typical. Ivy sighed and bit back her retort. Holly being helpful was still bossy and abrasive.

"Fine." The way this was starting, Ivy figured she'd need to keep her fingers crossed all day. She really hoped this fundraiser went off without a hitch. She knew how important it was to the historical society's projects and continued existence.

The drive out to Oleander House was spent with Holly talking up her own items and how fabulous they were. Ivy only half listened until Holly began to expound on how she had baked Ivy's special cookies.

*Hah, no you did not* was Ivy's first thought, but she politely nodded. Then her heart stuttered. Oh, dear, what if?

She began to breathe a bit faster. "So, Holly, how did you bake them?"

"What do you mean how? I do this for a living, just like you. I created a recipe based on your cookies. I've been perfecting it all week. It might not be *exactly* the same as yours, but it's certainly a close approximation. I know you'll never share your *oh-so-special* recipe." A big eye roll followed. "You're so secretive about the recipes that Mom gave you." Holly added an unhappy little sniff. "But I could taste what was in them. I do know how to back-engineer a recipe."

Holly creating her own recipe off of someone else's was Holly's speed. Once she had it mastered, or believed she had, she would never veer from it. But it wasn't only the recipe. How far was Holly willing to go to match Ivy's cookies?

Ivy bit her lip. She had to ask. "Did you use the cookie press?" Her words came out too high-pitched.

Holly cast her a catty-eyed glance. "Well, of course I used a cookie press. That's what makes them special."

Ivy's stomach did a little flip-flop, but they'd arrived.

Holly pulled up and parked and was out of the van with the doors open and setting boxes on a dolly to roll in before Ivy could even get her bearings. Her head was reeling at the thought of Holly using the antique cookie press. They'd both grown up hearing the legend of it, even if Holly put no credence into it.

But if Holly hadn't matched the recipe exactly, it would be okay, right? Or, did the recipe even really matter? Ivy had added nutmeg, lots of nutmeg, and the cookies worked. Maybe the magic wasn't in the recipe at all. Maybe it was all in the cookie press.

Holly having new devoted customers would be okay, right? Ivy had, after Jaxon shared his tin of cookies. Maybe Holly would find her own happily ever after. Just because it hadn't worked out for Ivy didn't mean it wouldn't work out for her sister. That would be good, wouldn't it? A happy Holly would be better for everyone.

Ivy's head was spinning by the time Malory hastened out to greet them and direct them where to set up. Ivy trailed behind the two of them through the mansion, taking in the lovely décor. Holly didn't spare it a glance, but Ivy paused to soak it in.

She stopped in front of the china cabinet as she passed and noted that some of the larger serving platters had been removed. Had Malory set them out to use? Ivy clapped her hands a little in an imitation of her aunt Lydia. She hurried to catch up and was delighted by her first glimpse of the courtyard. It wasn't fully enclosed, but the coach house and towering oleanders in the back made it feel protected, cozy, and a world apart. The coach house was open, displaying an antique carriage. Really, where did Malory find all these items? With the coach house to the east, it sheltered them from most of the wind coming off the coast.

The landscaping was flawless, but with Malory in charge the gardeners had likely been doubly inspired to perfection. The oleanders in the courtyard concerned Ivy. Green lawns edged by blue hydrangeas in full bloom beside an abundance of pink and yellow long-stemmed rosebushes, though, were lovely. Long tables were covered in white linen tablecloths with the china platters set out.

"Oh, I'll set the baked goods on the platters," Ivy volunteered. She gave a little pleased jump at the thought. First, she set out her souvenir tea packets with her Georgian Colonial blend. Next, she chose the two prettiest platters to display her sweet and savory items and arranged the pastries in their sleeves to the side for guests to take. Seeing Ivy's approach, Holly did the same.

Ivy was almost afraid to turn and see Holly's cookies pressed with the floral design she had become so familiar with, but she had to know. Bravely, she primed herself to look. She blinked. "What's this?" She waved a hand at Holly's oversized cookies.

"Aren't they splendid?" The four-inch diameter cookies were pressed with the words Hollister's Bakery in swirling calligraphic script. "I had my own cookie press designed. It's better since it advertises while also being pretty, and it's easy to read. See, you can learn from me. You don't have to always use some old antique. You can modernize and market your business. Make a note."

"Yes, it's very clever. You're so clever, Holly. What a great idea." Ivy let out a relieved breath. Her stomach untwisted, knowing the antique cookie press was safe, that magic cookies were not being indiscriminately passed out to the Hazard community.

*Again.*

Ivy had never intended for that to happen. That had been all Jaxon. This time, she was being careful. Her magic cookies were safely locked up in her shop, waiting for a perfectly controlled opportunity to share them with Jaxon.

No more mistakes.

Ivy crossed her fingers and smiled. She reached into the bottom of the large plastic bin with her items and caught her breath.

*No, no, no, it couldn't be.*

She knew what she was seeing.

The magic cookies in their plain white box tied with her signature green ribbon stared back up at her.

Holly had brought them along, or one of her employees had. It absolutely didn't matter how they got here. Ivy knew she couldn't serve them at this event. They needed to go back to her shop—now. Maybe she could slip away and drive them back.

Except she didn't have her own car. And she couldn't explain it to Holly.

"Hand those to me. I'll put them out." Holly took hold of the white bakery box. Ivy gripped it tight. A tug of war ensued.

"What is wrong with you?" said Holly.

"These aren't for today," Ivy hissed.

"They're cookies, right? I can see through the clear part. They won't keep. I know you didn't bake them last night. The box is cool, and cookies are only good for a few days."

"Well, maybe they're too old, then."

"If they're not fit to serve, I'll toss them."

Ivy couldn't bear the thought. "It isn't that. Please, Holly, these cookies shouldn't have come. Don't be difficult."

"Fine, put them in the van." Holly sniffed, pulled her keys from her pocket, and dangled them in Ivy's face.

Ivy hesitated. She could lock the cookies in the van, but Holly would want her keys back, leaving the cookies out of Ivy's direct control. "I'll just tuck them away—somewhere. She glanced about wildly. Where could she store them that was safe?

She couldn't put them under the tables on the grass. They might get ruined. She didn't dare set them on a table. They might get eaten. The coach house, maybe. She could hide them.

Malory plucked the box away from both of them. "If

they aren't for the event, I'll place them in the kitchen hutch. How's that? No one would presume to remove them. Guests won't be in the kitchen. Honestly." With an eye roll, Malory took the cookies. Ivy could hardly go running after her without looking ridiculous. Holly was already staring.

She tried nonchalance. "Okeydokey."

"Is it?" Holly's eyes narrowed in speculation.

"Of course."

But Holly wasn't having it. "What's really going on? Spill, little sis."

"Nothing to spill. I made those for"—Ivy decided she might as well be honest—"Jaxon."

"Tell me you're not still stalking our intrepid landlord."

"Not stalking, really, Holly!"

"You know he's not right for you. Oh, he looks good and all that, but he doesn't have any staying power."

"What's that supposed to mean?"

Holly tightened her lips and turned away.

But this time, Ivy was having none of it. She grabbed Holly's arm and tugged until her sister spun back to face her. "You spill."

"Doesn't matter," mumbled Holly, not meeting her eyes.

The four pillars arrived together then, in their way, requiring everyone's immediate notice. Seymour loped into the courtyard from the back, voice raised in disagreement with Aunt Lydia, who rushed in her brusque, take-charge way while Marjorie fluttered about trying to mediate. Hazel was teetering, and Ivy rushed to lend a hand to the president of the Hazard Historical Society. She knew Holly was hiding something, but Holly knowing secrets about Jaxon made zero sense and would have to be unraveled later.

Somehow, in the midst of getting everything situated, Holly wound up serving at the punch table with Ivy clear across the courtyard at the champagne table filling glasses and setting them out for the arriving guests. She'd need to pump Holly for information about Jaxon later.

Ivy passed out champagne flutes to members of the community, making small talk. She was pleased to see so many of the merchants on the square. Cece, her hair bleached a dark orange today and styled in cornrows, arrived with her looming husband Dart, bringing along Kate Mayfield, the new owner of the Hazard Inn. Ivy greeted Toby and Mackenna, who showed up with her rival from the chocolate shop Celestina's across the square. Celeste had a competitive gleam in her eye as she scrutinized the baked goods in the sleeves advertising their businesses.

A musical quartet played fife and drums in lively historical tunes, and the guests applauded. The downstairs was opened for guests to wander through the rooms and see what they were supporting.

Ivy had just relaxed into her role when she glanced up to find Jaxon across from her.

"May I?" he asked.

Her heart pounded. He was here and looking so—Jaxon.

Her mind flitted to the cookies stashed in the kitchen, but she shook her head slightly. This was not the time. Too many variables. Knowing Jaxon, he'd offer them around to everyone.

"No?" He gave her a wry smile. "I can't have any champagne."

"What, oh, of course you can." She handed him a glass and their fingers touched, sending a little thrill through her. Jaxon was all dressed up today, very debonair in a suit coat with a tie and jeans. Well, not too dressed up, more casual formal.

He shrugged. "I never know what to wear to these events. Will you join me?" Jaxon motioned over one of the servers circling with trays of empties. "Can you take over for a moment here, so Ivy can enjoy the event?" He took her hand in his, drawing her away. He tucked her hand into his arm. They fell into step easily, enjoying the garden around them, stopping to chat with other guests, a few of them visitors to the area, several from neighboring Newport. The wind began to kick up, churning the bushes around them. She and Jaxon moved into the shade. At a strong gust shaking the shrubbery, a piece of oleander twig fell into his champagne glass. As he raised his glass to his lips, Ivy dashed it from his hand, the glass shattering on the bark-lined path.

At his shocked expression, Ivy hastened to explain. "The oleander, it fell..." Malory was there immediately with a server to clean it up along with reproachful frowns for Ivy.

"It was the oleander. I couldn't let him drink it."

Malory was all business, but Ivy could tell she was irked at the broken glassware.

Jaxon drew her away from Malory's ire to whisk her inside. "Thank you for saving me."

He was amused, but really, it could have been deadly. Ivy understood now how easily her ancestor had died from oleander-contaminated tea. Perhaps she should send Rob to talk to the historical society about increasing their general liability coverage.

But Jaxon was drawing her away and her heart was racing now at his proximity and attention. Together, they wandered the downstairs. She knew Jaxon had consulted with Malory on the restoration of the house, and she asked him questions as they walked. He pointed out various architectural details she might otherwise have missed, and she shared with him the history of her ancestor's journey from France to settle in the new world.

"Well, I for one am glad he survived his travails and married, even though he lost his first love. If he hadn't, you wouldn't be here, with me, today." They stepped around the dining table to a shadowed alcove near the buffet.

He turned her to face him and took both her hands in his. As she gazed up at him, he gave a gentle smile and leaned in. Their lips met in a soft, sweet kiss that made Ivy's heart pound even as she caught her breath, here in the home of her ancestors, with the history of Hazard all around. Making new memories, with new hope, her heart soared. She belonged in Jaxon's arms.

"Oh, there you are."

Ivy jumped and turned to see Aunt Lydia enter the drawing room before realizing her aunt's comment wasn't directed at them when she started chatting with Cece. Neither Lydia nor Cece had seen them, but Jaxon distanced himself, and Ivy regretted the loss of their closeness. When they were still unnoticed, he placed his hand on Ivy's back as if to guide her from the room.

Cece was nodding, saying, "I wish I could move my salon to a beautiful location like this. I wonder if any of these historical old buildings will ever open up for businesses and not just tours. That would be something."

"Did you check with Kate, the new owner of the Hazard Inn? She has lots of downstairs space she might rent out if she only plans to have hotel rooms on the higher floors. Do you foresee relocating your business?"

"Well, we don't have much choice, do we? What with all the changes, I'm keeping my options open. You never know with a new landlord."

Lydia was nodding sagely.

"New landlord?" Ivy said to Cece, and glanced at Jaxon. *Why did he act guilty?* "What are they talking about?"

"Jaxon is selling the building, dear." Lydia spoke with clear condemnation.

"Haven't you told her, yet?" said Cece, in amazement.

"Really, Jax, bad form."

"What are they talking about?" Ivy repeated at Jaxon, who shifted backwards, farther from her.

As if swallowing bile, his words came out choked. "I'm...selling the building."

Ivy took a step toward him. "We negotiated a new lease. Why didn't you say something? Wait, does everyone know except me?"

He shook his head. "I'm so sorry."

Cece tsked.

Dart walked up. "When does your cool new job start in Boston, Jax? Great opportunity. I know how you can't wait to leave, but I'll sure miss seeing you walk that cute little dog. You've been a great neighbor. Sorry to see you go."

"Go?" Ivy repeated, feeling stupid and out of step. *Did everyone know Jaxon was leaving except for her?*

"Does Holly know?" she asked the room.

At Jaxon's chagrined expression, she pushed off from him. She needed to get away. Somewhere she could think.

Everything she'd accomplished paled if Jaxon left. If she had to move her successful tea shop, her uptick in business was for nothing. A rent increase to more than she could afford would drive her out of the town square, causing her business to drop off. She depended on walk-ins. Even if the new landlord honored her newly negotiated lease, and there was no guarantee of that, a year might not be enough to make relocating feasible. She'd invested so much money into decorating her current location. She'd been building her business, or thought she had. And now?

Really, what had she accomplished?

Jaxon had betrayed her. His dishonestly sabotaged her career.

"Why? Why couldn't you have told me?"

Holly popped in, and Ivy turned her ire on her sister. "You knew. All this time, you all knew he was leaving, and no one said a word to me."

The perfidy was too much. It was the story of her life—Ivy Wayland, always the last to know.

"Yes, well, it was Jaxon's place to say something, wasn't it?" Holly huffed. "You might as well give him that latest batch of the *Very Special Cookies* you baked as a going away present."

"Ha, you didn't," said Lydia in horror. "After we told you it was unwise?"

"Cookies?" said Jaxon, brow furrowed.

The mere thought of giving the man she loved her Very Special Cookies *now* after his betrayal was too much. Ivy balked. Giving magic cookies to a man who kept relevant truths was abhorrent. He didn't deserve them. He didn't deserve her.

The mere idea of him enjoying her magic cookies, inspiring his devotion, made heat rise in her cheeks. She didn't want devotion. She had the devotion of half the town. From Jaxon, she craved honesty, forthrightness, to be included in what he was willing to tell everyone but her.

Ivy fled.

In the foyer, she gripped the shiny brass doorknob on the towering front door, to jerk it wide, but it held. She tugged again and again, leaning her weight back, but it would only move an inch before slamming back closed, the wind from outside holding it shut, even as she struggled.

"Please," she murmured, "please, let me escape." The wind dropped. She flung the door wide, tripping backward as it slammed against the wall. Ivy dashed outside, air currents enveloping her, embracing her, hustling her down stone steps, past flowerpots, toward the towering shrubbery, urging her along, faster, faster, faster. She stumbled into the shade of the oleanders and stopped, breathless, nearly sobbing, to hide in the shadows.

Raindrops splattered, just a bit at first, small ones growing until they were plopping and splashing all around. Rain, promised by that red morning sky, arrived. It expanded, wind gusting its torrents. Ivy could hear the guests squealing at the sudden onslaught and scrambling for cover as the first Annual Hazard Historical Society Fundraiser came to an abrupt halt due to rain.

She should go help. She started to, but stopped and drew farther back into the oleanders. She couldn't bring herself to leave their shelter. They encircled her. She was safe here.

Usually she felt safe with Jaxon, but now? Now, she sought nature's shelter, here in her family's ancestral lands.

Here, in the heart of Hazard's countryside. Hazard was home, even here under the oleander bushes. Thick and towering, they protected her from the worst of the rain. She watched as the guests fled, running to cars, locks beeping open, windshield wipers pounding out the rhythm of the rain. Ivy began to hum the blessing. Peace fell over her like a blanket.

Even when she saw Holly pack up and drive away in the pink-and-white striped bakery van, casting one last glance around, calling on her cell phone, Ivy waited. Her cell was in the house, anyway. She couldn't answer if she wanted to.

And she didn't.

So she waited. She possessed no desire to drive off with Holly. Holly, who would lecture her like *she* was the one at fault, Holly who claimed she wanted to protect her but lied.

Ivy waited, even when it was Jaxon looking around, wondering where she had gone.

Let him wonder.

And when everyone had left but Malory, Ivy emerged from the bushes. The rain had stopped. The wind died down. She was damp but not dripping. Remarkable, really. She had always thought of oleanders as dangerous, poisonous plants, and they were, true, but they had sheltered her as their own.

"Thank you," she murmured.

She made her way toward the house as a car drove up, splashing through puddles, gravel crunching. A white rental sedan from the look of it, both doors popped open and her parents spilled out looking travel-worn.

Her parents? Here, now, really?

"Oh, darling," said her mother, as Ivy emerged from the bushes, twigs caught in her hair. "We came as soon as we could."

# Chapter Twenty-One

MALORY SERVED TEA to Ivy's parents in the formal dining room while Ivy dried her hair upstairs in what was apparently the family suites. She had no idea this even existed, but apparently there was a third floor accessible only to family and, well, Malory, of course. Ivy realized she could live here if she wanted. Amazing. She could certainly hide out here, at least for now. Though she would need her car. She did need to open the shop on Tuesday. No long-term hiding. It wasn't her style, anyway.

Ivy stepped down the grand staircase and listened outside the dining room while Malory told her parents about all the restoration done on Oleander House.

Ivy smoothed her dress and turned the corner. It had been months since she'd seen either of her parents. She noted her father's gingery hair had more white now than the faded red brown she remembered, but her mother looked the same, blonde hair in riotous curls around her face as she sat in the high-backed chair sipping delicately from a china teacup and making eyes with Ivy's father, who was smiling that smile he reserved only for her mother.

"Ah, there's my clinging ivy." Her father rose and opened his arms. Ivy gave both him and her mother a hug.

"We were just telling Malory how sorry we are to have missed the fundraiser. We'd hoped to make it on time."

It was humbling to realize what her mother's words meant. She hadn't been trying to get to Ivy as soon as she could. Why would she? She had no idea what her youngest was going through. Still, her mother's gaze on her was knowing, so perhaps she did sense something.

Her parents' magic might be fake, but her mother's intuition was unsurpassed.

Ivy basked in their presence and just sat, depleted, leaving Malory to clean up, who afterward handed off the keys to Ivy's parents. Ivy could see her brief struggle relinquishing control and was proud of Malory for entrusting her parents with Oleander House.

"Don't worry," her mother said. "We're magicians. We can fix anything." She flashed a sassy smile, and Malory even cracked a sheepish one of her own.

She nodded and left Oleander House in their care.

Ivy's mom shooed her dad upstairs and turned to her daughter. "Tell me."

Ivy unloaded on her mom all about Jaxon preparing to move and not telling her. She shared how Holly kept it a secret, and even Aunt Lydia said nothing, when they both knew how she felt. The only one clueless about her feelings was Jaxon.

"Is he though?" asked her mother.

Ivy gave a bleak shrug.

"Well, no fussing about it now. Your father and I need to practice our magic show, and you get to help. We're booked for next weekend at the Kite Jubilee. They decided to hold it again this year, what with all the wind we've been having. Marvelous, isn't it? I'm quite excited to perform in Hazard. And, of course, your father and I will need a kitchen for our anniversary tomorrow to bake our Very Special Cookies. You have the antique cookie press tucked away, I assume."

"It's hanging in the shop. Whenever I use it, everything goes wrong."

"Does it? I'm not sure that's possible. You did add nutmeg, didn't you, when you baked yours?"

Ivy nodded.

"I knew you would."

"It isn't in the recipe."

"Well, of course not, not everything is written down."

"How was I supposed to know?"

"You did know." Her mother shrugged. "I knew you would. Honestly, darling, when it's important, you just know. I knew with your father."

"Knew what?"

"That he's the one. I baked the cookies and used the press and here you are."

"Mom, you aren't making sense. I used the cookie press and now an entire baseball team is devoted to me. The second batch that I baked for Jaxon got eaten by Holly. And the third batch…"

Ivy's mother raised an eyebrow.

"Oh, you think this time it will work?" Hope blossomed in Ivy for one second before she remembered what Jaxon had done.

"The magic of Hazard never goes awry."

Ivy frowned at her mother.

"The magic of Hazard knows best."

Ivy shook her head. "I don't believe it."

"You don't have to. It still works. That's all part of the magic. Now, let me get a deck of cards, and you can help me practice for the jubilee."

Ivy rose to do her mother's bidding. On the way back, she peeked in the kitchen to confirm her cookies remained safely tucked in the hutch.

They had vanished.

# Chapter Twenty-Two

JAXON HAD ENOUGH. He couldn't wait to leave Hazard. He hadn't been able to bear telling Ivy the truth about leaving, and *she* took that as a slight. Seriously, he'd tried to spare her. Let her be—what—happy?

Jaxon let out a grown. What had he been thinking?

He hadn't, that's all—at least not with his head. Of course she felt slighted. He let out a shuddering sigh. She was mad and rightly so. He might as well skip right on out of here. He had a job lined up. An apartment. He could design actual houses instead of small remodels. So what if they were unimaginative, cookie-cutter houses? Small and cramped and affordable. That's right, he was off to save the world by designing affordable housing.

Of course, his idea of an affordable house and his soon-to-be employer's idea were vastly different. He wouldn't be in charge. A job was a job, and it would further his career until he could make enough money to buy land to build his own not-so-affordable house. He needed a serious job, working for a serious corporation, to do that.

Was he selling out? Or being smart? Candace would've

said he was being smart. Unfortunately, she hadn't lived to see it.

Ivy would say—what?

He had a meeting with the Realtor to sign the final paperwork. To sell his building to Derrick Cross. He just needed to find his way.

---

IVY HAD DONE it. She had banished Jaxon Langford from her mind, and sampled her *signature* tea blend. It was better than Find Your Way. A touch sweet, a touch earthy, and a touch wholesome. A bit like herself. She never considered herself earthy before. But after Saturday's stint in the oleanders, she had a new rapport with nature. She was connected to the earth, safe, and at home on the planet.

She fretted over the mysteriously missing cookies. Even after quizzing Malory, she had no clue who took them.

She frowned. She just needed someone to test out her new concoction. Ah, here was a customer—a dark-haired, dark-eyed, classically handsome male. Her new bell tinkled when he walked into her shop—a repeat customer Ivy recognized from the other day. He was here and she was in business yet for a while.

"Welcome."

He gave an abrupt nod. She ushered him over to her favorite corner table in a little patch of sunlight with the best view of the square. Sunlight cast the man's features in sharp relief. He radiated danger, incongruous with such a handsome face.

"What can I get you today? I have a signature tea blend."

"Coffee."

Ivy shook her head. At his incredulity, she explained, "This is a tea shop."

"Fine, I'll try your signature whatever." At his impatient, dismissive gesture, Ivy decided to win him over. Her new blend really was extraordinary.

When Ivy brought it over on a tray, he ignored the sugar and cream and drank it straight. She had steeped it dark, as that brought out its aromatic earthiness. She stood back, confident. She had spoken the blessing over her blend while she mixed it.

He took a drink and coughed, "Ugh, what is this?"

"It's tea, my signature blend. It's…"

"Awful."

Ivy stood up straighter. "It—isn't." It wasn't. It really wasn't. It could only be awful to an awful person. She narrowed her eyes. She was through being intimidated by pushy people.

"Bring me something else, something more like coffee, something bitter."

She whisked the tray away, content not to waste her best creation on the undeserving. She brewed him a pot of boring orange pekoe, inferior to everything else in her shop, and placed it before him.

He ignored her and sipped. "Much better."

When Jaxon strolled into view—despite her annoyance with him, Ivy still was attuned to his presence in the vicinity—the man flung some bills on the table. He stopped Jaxon outside. Figures Jaxon would keep company with such a disagreeable individual.

Cece slipped in the door as the two men strode off down the street. "You know who that was, don't you?"

Ivy shook her head.

"Derrick Cross—our soon-to-be landlord."

*Oh no*, thought Ivy. *What have I done?* "Cece, could you try my new blend of tea and tell me what you think?" Ivy poured a cup and Cece took a sip.

"Oh my, that's enchanting. It's better than any tea blend I've ever had. Needs a touch of sugar, though. You know how I like my tea just the tiniest bit sweet." She added a generous dollop to her cup and stirred, the silver spoon tinkling pleasantly against the bone china. Cece took another swallow. "My goodness, the second sip is even better than the first. It's absolute perfection. What are you calling this charming creation?"

Ivy considered before settling on a name. "I'm calling it…Magical." She gave a decisive nod. "Because it brings out your true self."

JAXON WALKED WITH Derrick to the Realtor's office. Time to close the momentous deal he had labored toward for months. Finally, he'd be free to move on. So, why did it feel dreadful? Derrick Cross, soon to be sole owner of his building, didn't act any happier than he did. He acted perplexed, instead of his usual assertive self. Jaxon had seen him exit the tea shop. He wondered what it was about Derrick's experience that had left him quietly disconcerted. They spoke little on the way over. Which suited Jaxon fine. He needed time to think.

He glanced back at the tea shop, at Ivy framed by frilly lace curtains in her picture window, chatting with Cece and pouring tea from a flowered pot, sunlight glinting off her honey-toned hair. The scene beckoned, inviting him to realize all he'd lost. He almost turned back, but instead he lengthened his stride to keep in step with Derrick.

He'd made his decision, a choice that shattered his last chance with Ivy. So, fine, he would do right by himself.

They passed Hollister's Bakery with its long queue, patrons obediently taking a number to wait their turn for baked bread and pastries, birthday cakes, and pies. People celebrating joyful lives.

Keeping in stride, he passed Cece's Salon, stylists clipping and cutting, primping the population of Hazard into their best selves.

His own office came into view. Tiny and simple, he'd had good years designing kitchen remodels, garage apartments, and expansions for homes with growing families. He'd contributed to the community, made his mark, belonged.

Jaxon halted.

A yellow school bus full of kids rounded the corner. Boys he coached in Little League waved at him from the half-open windows. He raised a hand. Derrick scowled.

Jaxon remained glued to the sidewalk. If he accepted the Boston job, would he lose his joy, like Derrick? Why exactly was Derrick Cross so determined to buy up property in Hazard?

Not speaking, they crossed the street to the realty office. When the brunette receptionist gave a cheerful smile, Derrick turned on his charm. Jaxon recognized a man with a hidden agenda, and he wanted no part in it. He simply could not risk the livelihoods of his tenants. Not for a selfish move he no longer needed to make.

The complication was that he had accepted Derrick's offer on the property. All that remained was signing the final documents. If he didn't sign, what then? Would he be in breach of contract? The contract wasn't actually signed. He hadn't yet relinquished his rights to the property.

Jaxon turned to Derrick, who was bestowing his oily smile on the unsuspecting receptionist. Preening at his attention, the young woman ushered them into the thickly carpeted back office where the blazer-clad Realtor, Sally Song, waited with a bespectacled notary behind a polished teakwood desk.

Jaxon sat in a padded oxblood chair, a substantial stack of paperwork placed before him. He took his time to read through each page one last time. Even as his eyes flowed over the words, his life in Hazard replayed in his mind. When had he begun to belong? How had he not realized?

Derrick Cross shifted in impatience, his sneering lips pinched closed, somehow knowing now was not the time to push. Over the page in his hand, Jaxon studied the man he'd once thought was the answer to his dreams. Derrick Cross, moneyed, well-dressed, rigid, harsh, secretive. How had he ever thought he could work with him? How had he ever thought to foist this discontented man on his friends and neighbors?

On Ivy.

"Deal's off."

Derrick swiveled in his direction, all oily charm evaporated. "You can't do that."

"I'm not selling. I've changed my mind."

"We have an agreement. The *notary* is here."

Jaxon stood, took the paperwork in hand, and looked Derrick straight in the eyes. "No deal."

Derrick grabbed for the paperwork. Jaxon held it. Keeping his gaze on Derrick, he deliberately tore the documents in half.

Derrick Cross narrowed his eyes. "You know what this means."

Jaxon raised an eyebrow.

"I'll find another piece of property. Little by little, I will buy up this wretched town and transform it. I'll wrest it out of its revolting past and force it into this century. I'll bring in modern businesses that people want to patronize and force out all those horrible mom-and-pop shops."

"Those mom-and-pop shops are the charm of Hazard."

Derrick scoffed, "I'll turn this place into a profitable enterprise, not this century's old, closed club. It'll be…"

"…like everywhere else?"

"That's right." Lip curling, Derrick glowered.

"You'll fail."

"You watch." He pivoted abruptly but halted at the door. "Oh, and Langford, you can consider your new position terminated. You cancel this sale…your job offer?" Derrick made a sign with his fingers of it going up in smoke. "Good luck with your life here for as long as that lasts."

Derrick stormed out, and Jaxon turned to the Realtor. "Sorry about your commission."

Sally shrugged. "I just completed the sale on the Hazard Inn. I'll be all right."

Jaxon nodded to her and the notary, and left. Time to put his life back together.

# Chapter Twenty-Three

CROWDS GATHERED AND milled about Cliffside Park. Ivy adored this event. It had been canceled for the last couple of years. But the Kite Jubilee was back, and due to recent high, gusting winds, today was the ideal, blustery day for kite-flying. A stage had been set up for her parents to perform their magic show, and afterward would be a live band for dancing. It didn't get any better than this.

Except Jaxon was leaving. That thought remained in the back of her mind as she went through her busy days. Yes, the tea shop was thriving. She'd improved her business nearly 30%, but the knowledge Jaxon was leaving dimmed her joy.

Rumor had it the sale of his building had fallen through, but Ivy had barely seen Jaxon all week. No one had. That meant he was still moving, taking a job in Boston, and leaving Hazard behind. Jaxon Langford was leaving her behind, and that was fine because he had betrayed her.

Except, if it was true, and he wasn't selling the building, he hadn't—not exactly. True, he held back important information. He'd left her out when he talked to everyone else. That irked, but it wasn't a genuine betrayal. He *was* still her landlord, so they *would* still be in touch.

Ivy wasn't sure how she felt about that.

She shoved the turmoil from her mind. Too much to do today, and she needed to focus on each task at hand. She and Holly had a vendor booth together. Ivy had packaged up her special tea blends—Serenity, Cozy, Find Your Way. She hadn't packaged any of the Magical blend. That was only for the tea shop. She was learning from Holly. To have the very best of her blends, you had to come into the shop to experience it. Magical had already grown in popularity and was the most ordered blend in the shop. Well, among the pleasant customers. The unpleasant customers couldn't abide it. It really did bring out a person's inner attitude. Bad attitude, bad taste. Great attitude, great taste.

The youngest of the kite flyers were already letting out their strings with diamond shapes fluttering merrily in the breeze. Parents were overseeing the activity and keeping their youngsters away from the perilous drop to the ocean. Cliffside was Ivy's favorite place to walk. She loved the windy path, with a view of the surf crashing below.

She paused to watch the kite flyers and caught her breath. Jaxon in the afternoon, with the breeze ruffling his hair, always caught her just a little unawares. He stood in the midst of it all. Of course, he did. He was helping his Little Leaguers fly their kites: deltas and parafoils in a rainbow of colors. She watched as he helped Ronnie's younger brother get his kite swaying and looping in the air.

Crowds were gathering as her parents began their show. First, card tricks with giant cards added a touch of humor. She could hear gasps and oohs as they performed their illusions, scarves and lop-eared bunnies appearing out of top hats and teapots. The teapots had been her idea, and her parents loved it. It gave her business a plug before they moved onto their disappearing act. Holly scowled.

Ivy ignored her sister and focused on her booth and the customers. She tried to avoid looking at Jaxon. She was not. She was *not* looking at him. She was looking somewhere else, except somehow, he had moved straight into her line of vision. If she looked away it would be silly, wouldn't it?

"I can see you watching him and pretending you aren't," said Holly. "It's so obvious."

"It is not," Ivy murmured, and began straightening her tea packages.

"Is to."

"Is not." What were they, eight? Just because their parents were visiting didn't mean they needed to resort to grammar school behavior.

"You can go over. I'll watch the booth."

"You'll put all your items in the front and mine under the table."

"Hah." Holly widened her eyes in mock shock, then grinned. "Maybe."

Rebecca chose that moment to wander over. "Do you ever need help in your tea shop? My dad says I have to get a job when I turn sixteen."

Ivy opened her mouth to answer, when Holly talked over her. "Why don't you find out if you'd like it? You can take Ivy's spot while she steps away. Go," Holly said to her sister, and made a shooing motion. "Go over to the kite flyers. I know you want to."

She did. She really did.

"Becca will be my helper."

Becca gave a pleased jump. "Can I?"

Ivy untied her green apron embroidered with the Ivy Way Tea Shop in elegant script and handed it to the excited teen to put on. She pointed her finger at her sister. "Don't hide my product." To Becca, she said, "Don't let her hide my product." Holly laughed, and they both waved her off.

As Ivy stepped away from the shelter of the vendor section, her light, flower-print dress began to flap against her legs, and she was glad she'd thought to put on shorts under it. She passed Malory, who was struggling with an elaborate dragon kite while simultaneously trying to keep her full skirt from flying up behind. Malory grumbled, but when she spotted Ivy, she shoved the kite string into her hands. "I can't do this. My skirt almost blew all the way up in back. I refuse to flash these people. I must maintain my decorum."

Ivy grinned at Malory's consternation and took the string. "I wanted a kite to fly. How did you know?"

"Good luck with it. This wind's too strong. Someone's going to get hurt, tripping over themselves to keep up with their kite."

"Oh, it's not that bad. Let's move over to the kite-flying section in the meadow." Ivy nodded toward where Jaxon was helping the kids. "See, it's all safe. It isn't anywhere near the cliff's edge. They even have it roped off." She paused to watch Montgomery jump and dance his happy doggy dance around Jaxon, who was helping another Little Leaguer get his kite launched, demonstrating how to catch the best breeze.

"Oh, oh my," said Ivy, as the kite gave a tug and Malory's dilemma became clear.

"See what I mean?"

Ivy nodded and moved to the edge of the kite area. She loved watching the kite with its long dragon tail dip and rise and loop and turn. Dancing high above her like a live creature with a mind of its own, the fiery breath of her dragon kite was reminiscent of an apatosaurus in action. Ivy figured she had the coolest kite. Most of the kites for the youngsters were traditional diamond racers, but Ronnie's had a box shape that caught the wind even better than Malory's dragon. Ivy moved closer to the main section, closer to Jaxon.

Most of the participants were winding their strings in and heading toward the stage, bringing their kites back down to earth as her parents' magic performance grew more interesting. Ah, her dad was sawing her mom in half now. So clearly a trick of mirrors. Ivy sighed. A classic, really, and a crowd-pleaser with the younger audience.

Ivy watched her kite, half-watched her parents, and kept an eye on Jaxon as she hummed the blessing. The tune caught on the wind, and she began to sway and move with her kite. She wouldn't let Malory's fiery dragon take wing on its own. She found she agreed with Malory that flying kites near the cliff would be hazardous. If she walked the path later, it would be sans kite.

The dragon gave a sharp tug, trying to escape. Kids were heading in. She saw Jaxon move out of the roped-off section and turn the kids he was helping back over to their parents. Jaxon sent Ronnie's little brother off with him and watched until they were seated at the benches watching her mother disappear. The crowd applauded wildly. Jaxon caught her eye. She raised a hand to wave. But he had looked down to hook a leash onto Montgomery's collar. They were off on a walk.

Her heart ached to go after him, but Jaxon was heading toward the cliff to walk the path with his dog. Ivy continued holding onto the kite strings, but it felt like her heartstrings were tugging and whipping about, now looping in a nauseating fashion. She reminded herself that Jaxon had kept things from her, but all she longed to do was chase after him. Running toward the cliff in the strong wind was a decidedly bad idea. She began to reel the kite in.

Holly would grow impatient at her being away or annoyed at selling her product—or worse, hide it—and

Rebecca might get bored helping, so she figured she should head back. She carefully wound the string in, taking care not to damage Malory's dramatic kite. Once it was in control she found her friend, who took it back with a frown.

"You're better with it than I am."

"Well, we flew kites when I was a kid. It was windy then, too. I loved it. The wind calls to me. I'm right at home on a blustery day."

Malory shivered, even though the day wasn't cold. "I guess I'll get used to it. I'm more of an indoor girl." She rose to go stash her kite in her car, and Ivy headed back toward the magic show. It was in the height of it now with oohs and ahs at the grand finale. A kind of flash explosion hit in which all the items from earlier appeared and disappeared again, including her mom.

Wind was whipping strongly when she spotted a small figure off in the distance. Was that Ronnie's little brother? And what was he dragging behind him? It seemed to be wrapped about his legs. Ivy headed in that direction, trying to see what he was up to. He paused and appeared to throw something in the air. Ivy's ponytail whipped into her face, and she shoved it aside. It was a kite. But not the small racer he'd had earlier when Jaxon was helping him. This was the larger box kite of Ronnie's that really caught the breeze.

As she watched, it rose and looped and swung higher as the little boy let out the string, jumping up and down, running into the big open field away from the magic show and in the opposite direction from the roped-off safety zone.

Ivy dashed after him. He was headed toward the cliffs, air currents pulling him closer to the edge. Wind blasted her face as she shoved her now loose hair back to see.

She was too far away. Suddenly, Montgomery came bounding toward the boy, leash dragging.

*Where was Jaxon?*

Ivy ran faster. She called out, but she didn't know the boy's name. It was too late to enlist other help. She needed to catch him. The colorful box kite flew high, perilously swinging the boy up off the ground a few inches.

Ivy's legs pumped faster. She stumbled on the uneven ground, twisting her foot, but ignored the pain. The boy was struggling in the gale, forced closer and closer to the cliff edge. She yelled, but her voice flew off into the air. She screamed at the boy, but the wind was tumbling him toward the cliff, the kite dragging him to the edge.

Sound carried from the show with the repeated explosive popping of the finale, crowd cheering enthusiastically, marveling at her parents' creativity.

Montgomery was dashing in and out around the boy's feet, trying to hold him back, but they were both nearing the edge. Ivy was so close, if she could just reach him. With an extra burst of energy she leaped up, the wind giving her a boost toward the boy. She grabbed him up and swung him back from the cliff edge. She took the kite in hand, winding the string quickly. She'd done it. Dog and boy were safe.

"Are you all right?"

Eyes wide, his little body trembling, he nodded.

"Here, I'll bring the kite back. This wind's too high to be near the cliff with a kite. You go on back to your folks, ok? Take Montgomery." She handed the leash to the boy and Montgomery, good dog that he was, pulled the boy to safety. Ivy watched as they made it back to the crowd. Relieved, she stepped away from the cliff, but a draft caught the kite and she stumbled.

Her feet slipped as the earth slid out from under her. She fell, trying to reel the kite back in, but the wind was working against her, tugging the kite closer to the ocean. Ivy was on her hands and knees now. Afraid to stand in the strong gusts while holding a kite, she began to crawl, inching from the edge.

The ground shifted, gave way, and she released the kite. It took off in a wide swirling arc, heading over the sea and up to the clouds. Ivy sunk her fingers into the earth, but she was skidding over the edge. Surely there was a ledge she could grasp hold of, but her hands fumbled. As she dropped into free fall, she grabbed for a root protruding from the cliff, and held on.

Her feet dangled.

She scrambled, trying to find anything to grip onto. With her right hand, she grappled at the rock face and sunk her fingers into a crevice. Her feet caught on the side of the cliff, and she plastered herself like a bug on a wall.

Had anyone seen her go over the edge?

Anyone at all?

---

Jaxon cursed his dog. Montgomery had gotten loose from him again. Fortunately, his dog was so low to the ground that he wouldn't be swept off in these crazy gusts, Jaxon hoped. He came around the rise and spotted Montgomery leading a boy across the wide-open field. Was that Ronnie's little brother?

The boy halted, jumping and pointing back toward the cliff. "Jaxon, help," he called. His little voice flew on the air, but Jaxon just heard him. "She fell!"

*Fell? Who?* Jaxon ran toward the drop-off. The crowd began to sense a commotion. Nell and her friends from the Roadies were heading their way. Ronnie grabbed his little brother's hand just as their parents came running up.

He was pointing and explaining something, but Jaxon wasn't waiting for details. He ran toward the edge. If someone fell off a cliff—if anyone fell, he couldn't be right here where it happened—again.

His mind blanked. He couldn't do it. He couldn't stare down at a person, bleeding, broken, dead. His mind screamed to let the authorities handle it. But his heart pounded, urging him to run faster. Drawn closer to the edge, images of his worst failure flowed through his mind. He couldn't bring himself *not* to see, *not* to look, *not* to know.

He heard a small cry and a curse, and forced himself to peer over the edge. His stomach dropped to his toes. Terror froze him, but he shoved it back and sprang into action.

Ivy, his lovely, beloved Ivy, clung to the side of the cliff, her wide eyes fearful.

Jaxon dropped to the ground and lay down. He stretched over the edge. "Take my hands."

She shook her head, tears streaming down her cheeks. "No," she breathed.

"I'll pull you up and back."

"I can't." She turned to glance down and immediately turned terror-filled eyes back at Jaxon.

He kept his voice steady, encouraging. "You won't. I won't let you. I'm really strong. Here, take one of my hands."

The root she hung onto with her right hand began to creak and give, dirt scattering. Her left-hand grip tightened on the rock face, her fingernails breaking. He stretched his arm down, angling until she might just be able to reach his fingers. With a determined grimace, she let go of the root and snatched at the proffered hand. She missed on the first try, and swung to the left. She squealed, and Jaxon's heart stopped before pounding erratically. Keeping his focus on Ivy, he eased himself out farther. If the ground gave way, they'd plummet onto the rocks below.

Hands gripped his legs. "We've got you, Jax," he heard

Nell say. He eased farther, just a little bit farther, until Ivy could just grasp his fingers. "More," he told Nell.

"You heard him," she said. Jaxon felt another pair of hands. Someone else slipped a rope around his waist and tightened it.

"We won't let you fall," he heard Roman say.

Jaxon was hanging over the edge now, his fate in the hands of Hazard. He could hear the Roadies and the Rebels working together to help him rescue Ivy, easing him down until he gripped her wrist and she gripped his.

He heard a cheer from Joel. "You've got your girl. Don't let her go."

Jaxon pulled and kept his eyes on Ivy's. "Focus on me. You can do this." He gave her wrist an encouraging tug, and she let go of the rock face with her other hand. For one chilling instant she swung perilously, and if it weren't for the community holding onto Jaxon, he knew they would've tumbled into oblivion.

Jaxon grabbed Ivy's other wrist and began to pull her up as the others pulled him back, a combined team effort pulling them free from danger.

They weren't in this alone. He had Ivy, and the community had him. They all pulled and eased Ivy up and over the side.

She crawled the last little bit and, both on their knees, Jaxon pulled her into his arms. She clung. Nothing ever felt so right. She belonged in his arms. He belonged with her.

"I've got you. I've got you. I've got you." He couldn't stop repeating himself. "I've got you."

"I know," she answered, humor in her voice along with something else. He leaned back to search her eyes, expecting gratitude, but it was so much more. Love for him shone from her eyes. He hadn't lost her. His heart stuttered and steadied. He smiled, and she smiled, and while everyone milled around shouting instructions and sounding important, the two of them gazed at each other.

"I couldn't let you fall."

"You didn't."

"I love you."

She smiled the smile that warmed him all the way from his head to his toes. Ivy Wayland was sunshine personified. "Love you, too. Don't leave me."

"Never," he breathed, and drew her in for a kiss to seal his promise, while Montgomery did his happy little dog dance all around.

# Chapter Twenty-Four

IVY SAT WITH a blanket around her shoulders. The wind hadn't let up, and kites flew overhead but only in the roped-off safety arena with parents alertly supervising their children. Ivy perched on a wooden picnic table in the gazebo Jaxon had designed for Cliffside Park. She sipped tea from a large pink mug with Hollister's Bakery displayed on it in giant letters. Holly had fussed over her—as had her parents, until she had successfully waved them away. They had finally got the hint that she wanted to be alone with Jaxon.

Many of the others, the Roadies and the Rebels together, had left for a drink at Toby and Mac's. The pillars were already discussing the tale of the rescue of Ivy Wayland. Ivy was simultaneously thrilled and dreading the retelling, certain that it was destined to live on in Hazard lore.

Vendors were packing up their tables. Holly had a steadfast helper today in the form of Rebecca, but it was clear Becca preferred the tea shop to the bakery. It might be time to hire a helper, but first she needed to come clean to Jaxon. "I have a confession."

"A confession? Don't tell me you jumped off a cliff because you couldn't live without me." He grinned and tugged on a lock of her hair, still loose around her face.

"Oh, no. Not that. I would never admit to that."

"Let me guess, you thought you were a kite."

Ivy pinched her lips together and shook her head. His jovial mood was wonderful, but it wasn't making this any easier.

"Hmm, okay, how about…"

Ivy put her finger over his lips. He stopped, eyes dancing, waiting for her to speak.

"I tricked you. Or tried to. I know how bad that is. How wrong."

"Tricked me, how?" His arms moved around to hold her.

"I tried to trick you into loving me. I—oh, and this is the worst part—I baked magic cookies."

Jaxon blinked. He nodded thoughtfully, lips pursed. "Okay, I wouldn't have guessed that, but it's probably better than believing you're a kite." He grinned.

"Stop. You aren't taking me seriously. This is serious."

He laughed. "No, it's not. Your parents' show aside, there is no such thing as magic. And, as much as I love everything you bake, there is certainly no such thing as magic"—he wiggled his fingers in the air—"cookies."

"But there is. That's what I'm trying to tell you. It's a secret family recipe. It's why my parents love each other so much after all these years."

Jaxon was shaking his head. "I think they just love each

other, Ivy."

"But they bake the magic cookies every year, and they share them. I wanted that. I wanted what they have with each other." She gazed into his eyes. "I wanted to have that with you, so I baked the cookies. I followed the recipe exactly right." Remembering the added nutmeg, she crossed her fingers. "And I used the antique cookie press, so I could win the devotion of the recipient of the cookies, just like the legend says. And I"—she turned her gaze skyward before bringing it back to Jaxon's face—"gave them to you hoping you would see me, really see me for who I am."

Jaxon grinned "Really? Well, as flattering as that is…"

Ivy cut him off, "And then, you," she poked him in the chest, "shared them with the Rebels baseball team, and they all became devoted to me and started coming into the tea shop."

"That's probably because your cookies are fabulous."

"Because they're magic." At his skeptical laugh, she said, "You don't believe me."

He tilted his head. "Well, if your cookies are magical, so is your tea shop, but that's only because *you* are magic. You, Ivy, have brought the magic back into my life."

"But it's more than that."

He kissed her quick on the lips, once, twice.

She kissed him back a third time and gave him a light push. "It gets worse. When it didn't work the first time, I baked them again."

His eyes were laughing at her, and she loved it, but she needed to make him understand. She refused to deceive him. From now on, they'd agreed to be honest with each other.

"What happened to the second batch, because I don't remember getting any of these cookies. Wait, is that part of the magic?"

"No." She shoved him. "Holly ate them and started acting nice to me."

"Are you sure? Because that's kind of out of character for Holly."

"I told you, the magic is real."

"I'm not so sure. Holly wasn't very nice to you today."

Ivy waved that away and held up the mug. "She gave me a hot mug of tea and tucked a blanket around me."

"Yeah, but I think she also hid your scones under the vendor table to sell more doughnuts."

"I knew it! But that's not important, there's more. When the first two batches didn't work, I baked the magic cookies a third time."

"Oh, and who ate those?"

"They went missing from Oleander House."

He was grinning openly at her now, and she wanted to smack him and hug him all at the same time. When he finally settled down, he tucked her in close to him and said, "So let me get this straight. You use the cookie press, bake the magic cookies, and give them to someone, making them irrevocably charmed by you."

"That's right."

"Hmm."

"But it didn't work."

"No?"

"Because you never ate them, not one single cookie, not one single crumb."

"Let me be honest, now. I was upset by that."

"By me trying to trick you?"

He shook his head. "I wanted to eat your cookies. They smelled amazing, but when I didn't get any, it wasn't important. The cookies aren't important."

"They are."

"Oh, Ivy, don't you realize? I may not believe in magic cookies, but even if you do, I didn't need to eat a cookie to fall in love with you. I love it here in Hazard now because you're here, and the community bands together to take care of its own. But I didn't need the magic of Hazard to fall in love with you."

Ivy blinked and stared at Jaxon in amazement. He had called it exactly right. "We didn't need the magic of Hazard to fall in love." Ivy breathed the words with a kind of wonder.

Jaxon shook his head. "I was completely charmed by you the very first time we met. The day you signed the lease for your tea shop, and shared your dreams for the space, I was enchanted by everything about you. And, later, when I stepped into your cozy tea shop, I was home because you were there. You make my world complete. I didn't need magic to fall in love with you. Not the magic of baked goods, not the magic of cookie presses, not even the magic of Hazard."

"Hazard is pretty great."

"But that's because of you. It's you, Ivy, just you. I am charmed by you."

# Chapter Twenty-Five

Ivy caught her breath. Sunlight cascaded in the windows, brightening her shop and her heart as Jaxon turned and walked backwards to wave as he passed on his way to take Montgomery out on their morning jaunt. She knew he would stop in for a blueberry scone and his favorite Earl Grey, hot, before he headed to Langford Architectural Enterprise to work on his new project for the Hazard Inn.

She let out a little sigh, wishing she could put her arms around him like she had earlier and…

"Focus," said a voice behind her.

Ivy jumped and blinked twice to bring herself back to reality.

"You have work to do. Remember, you have a long day ahead of you. You need to clean up for me today."

Ivy spun around to confront her sister. "I do not. In case you didn't notice, I am in a committed relationship." She waved toward her man and his dog circling the town green. The statue of Edwin Hazard, founder, rose up amidst the surrounding maple trees swaying in what was now a constant breeze. Ivy loved that it was never still, that magic swirled all around the community endlessly. It was her own secret contribution to a community that couldn't get enough of her scones, cookies, and special tea blends.

Holly rolled her eyes and bobbed her head from side to side. "Yes, everyone knows Ivette Wayland is in a committed relationship with Jaxon Langford."

"Which means you can clean up for me." Ivy gave a pleased little jump, ponytail bouncing, as she set about preparing a tea tray for the four pillars gathering at their usual table. She had started putting a reserved sign on their table so that it would be available just for them.

Holly shook her head. "I ran all the tea shop's receipts from April and May, and the Ivy Way Tea Shop only improved its business 29.9%." Holly handed over a stack of spreadsheets she had printed out as proof, along with a broom. "You should start practicing."

Ivy stopped arranging pastries and put her hands on her hips. "You should round up."

"You should own up to your obligations."

Ivy opened her mouth to retort and closed it. She picked up the silver tea tray to carry out to her favorite customers. "You know what, you're right. I'll clean up your bakery mess all through June."

"You will?" Holly blinked at her sister.

Ivy nodded. She could be magnanimous. She had Jaxon. And Jaxon had her. Life was wondrous and astounding. But first: "Holly, I do have a favor to ask you before you head back to the bakery."

"Ha, here it comes. I knew you would try to get out of it."

"I won't. I swear. I just would really like you to try my new Magical tea blend."

"Oh, what's so magical about it?"

Ivy crossed her fingers. "It's just what I'm calling it. It's my signature blend."

"Oh, because your tea shop is magical now?"

Ivy kept her fingers crossed.

"That's it? You want me to try your tea blend?"

"I really want your impression of it." Ivy was dying to see whether Holly liked it or hated it. Really, she almost couldn't wait to find out. "It's already super popular with my customer base."

"Listen to you, trying to impress me by sounding like me."

Ivy beamed. "See, I am learning from you. So, will you do it? Will you try my new signature tea blend after work today?" At Holly's nod, she spun off with the tea tray to share the news with the Hazard Historical Society. They all loved her new blend and delighted in testing it out on others in the community.

"I love when you own up to your obligations, Ivy," Holly called after her.

"You bet!"

# Epilogue

*And even when it does start out magical, the Hazard Blessing has its own agenda...*

REBECCA WHITAKER HADN'T meant to eavesdrop, but by paying attention she had learned something valuable at Cliffside Park. She couldn't help but overhear what Ivy told Jaxon on the other side of the gazebo after the Kite Jubilee.

She peeked at the cookies tucked into her backpack. She'd come across the cookies at the Hazard Historical Society fundraiser. They had been stashed in the kitchen hutch in a plain white box, and she could swear they called to her.

She tried to ignore them. She knew they must belong to Ivy. They had that cute little green ribbon. She only took them out, so she could give them back to Ivy. She had borrowed her mom's shopping basket and tucked them inside and brought them to the Kite Jubilee to do the right thing. She'd finally worked up her nerve and gone by Ivy's vendor table, but Ivy took off to fly a kite and fell off a cliff and everything!

The worst part was, Becca didn't really *want* to give them back. She wanted them for herself, really, really a lot.

She ran her fingers over the clear window of the box. The cookies shimmered and whispered to her, oh so, so yummy.

Now, she knew exactly what to do. She wouldn't eat the cookies herself. She had a better plan. Now that she understood how the magic worked, she would sneak the cookies to the popular girls at school. She'd never been popular, and she wanted that. Because popular with her little brother's friends didn't count. She wanted to be popular like her mother. Her mother always talked about how great her high school years were. Becca wanted that. Since the cookies were hers now, all she had to do was share them with the popular girls and win their devotion.

Becca zipped up her backpack and ran her plan through her head as she walked to school. Today, she'd go to the student government assembly. She'd sit as close as she could to Jessica and Karysa and Marik with the open box and even inch it a tiny bit in their direction.

Because magic cookies were enthralling. How could they resist?

## The End

## *Acknowledgments*

Thank you to the amazing Tule Publishing team who took my idea for a single Christmas story and transformed it into the Charmed Love series, suggesting I base the first novel around a tea shop. From ideas to edits to beautiful covers, I can't imagine working with a better team.

Thank you to my husband and my grown children who have never failed to encourage me in my writing. Special thanks goes to my oldest daughter who beta read this story over a weekend, so I could make my deadline.

Thank you to my friends and coworkers, turned street team, for helping me shape my ideas, encouraging me throughout my process, and for always cheering me on.

And thank you to my amazingly talented writer friends, Jessica McBrayer, Karysa Faire, and Marik Berghs, who keep me on track with our weekend writing sprints. You are the popular girls!

*More Books by Aimee O' Brian*

**Steal My Heart**

## *About the Author*

Having lived in both California and Texas, Aimee O'Brian now resides in the beautiful wine country. With her three children grown and experiencing their own adventures, she and her husband are free to explore the world. When she's not reading, writing, or planting even more perennials in her garden, she can be found stomping through ancient ruins and getting lost in museums.

Thank you for reading

# The Magical Tea Shop

If you enjoyed this book, you can find more from all our great authors at TulePublishing.com, or from your favorite online retailer.

Made in the USA
Middletown, DE
27 January 2025